God's Keys

By

Ronna M. Bacon

ISBN 978-1-998821-31-0

Psalm 121:3. He will not allow your foot to slip; He who keeps you will not slumber.

Psalm 121:8 The Lord will guard your going out and your coming in rom this time forth and forever.

Psalm 91:3-7 For it is He who delivers you from the snare of the trapper And from the deadly pestilence. He will cover you with His pinions, And under His wings you may seek refuge; His faithfulness is a shield and bulwark. You will not be afraid of the terror by night, Or of the arrow that flies by day;

NKJV

Table of Contents

Chapter 1

The worn-out decrepit mansion hid in the shadows of the leafless trees and towering evergreens. Its weather-battered facade looked tired and old. The windows mostly filled with broken glass or empty of said glass gave the impression of unseeing eyes. The missing pickets on the porch railings seemed like a set of teeth that was not complete. The towering trees reached towards the sky, giving the impression of arms that were reaching for nowhere. The towering evergreens swayed slightly in the west wind that was blowing in off the lake, almost as if they were waving for help.

A small van, forest green in colour, pulled to a hesitant stop on the overgrown gravel driveway. The green on the side panels was interrupted by the name Cavanagh's Locks in descriptive script. A figure could be seen through the lightly tinted windows, just sitting and staring at the building.

The door to the van opened slowly and the figure dropped to the ground before dropping the keys to the van back onto the driver's seat. Surprisingly, it was a lady with her black hair caught back in a braid that ended near her waist. Cavanagh O'Rourke's keen aqua eyes studied the house and then the surrounding area. Why would anyone want to change the locks to this place, she questioned herself. She shuddered with fear for a moment. Cavanagh had never been in such a position. And she had to be the one to come. She owned the locksmith business now that had been started by her paternal grandfather, Dagen Cavanagh. Her father had taken it over when he started working and then had passed it on to her. Dagen worked in the shop now with her father unless they were needed on a job site.

Cavanagh sighed. This was not what she had expected. She muttered to herself as she turned in a circle, feeling that she was being watched. She didn't like that feeling. Her phone was clutched in her hand. Cavanagh was ready to call for help at any time. The old Lockyer mansion had been abandoned for years, with only the taxes paid on it.

Turning as she heard a vehicle approaching, Cavanagh reached for her van door handle, ready to jump in for safety. She frowned as she saw a surveyor's van approaching. What was happening here, Lord, she questioned. Why as a surveyor be out here? She had not heard that the property had been sold. And it certainly seemed too overgrown for a proper survey to be done by the single man in the vehicle.

Cleary O'Shea stared at the van and then the lady standing beside it. He could sense her fear and prayed that he had not been the one to scare her. He frowned as he studied the area, not sure why a lawyer had approached him and asked him to survey the property. The only stipulation had been that he do it on his own. Cleary had argued about that before he shrugged. God had not told him to avoid this place.

Cleary dropped to the ground, shutting the van door. He hesitated before he approached the lady. He pulled off his cap and ran his hand through his thick blond curls. His deep gray eyes studied her before he gave a grin.

"Hi. You're Cavanagh." He stopped about ten feet away from her.

"I am." Cavanagh frowned at him before she recognized him from church. "You're Cleary."

"That would be me. What are you doing here?" He gestured towards the house.

"I was asked to come out and change the locks. That doesn't make sense when the windows are broken out." Cavanagh turned back to face the house. "What are you doing here?"

"I was asked to do a survey and do it on my own. It's not possible to do that on my own as I was requested to do." Cleary walked towards the house with Cavanagh trailing after him. "Have you looked inside yet"

"No. I just got here. You weren't too far behind me." Cavanagh paused her forward walk. "I was told to be here at a certain time."

Cleary's steps hesitated before he turned to look at her. He frowned, thinking back through the emails that he had received. He had not spoken with the lawyer in person. Instead, all arrangements had been done through email. He had never questioned that.

"I was told to be here at a certain time as well. I wonder why." Clearly turned back to the house, carefully stepping up on the decrepit porch. He hesitated as the wood planks sank under his feet. They had been heavily damaged by the rain and snow over the years.

Cavanagh followed him, her steps on alternate planks to his. She drew in a deep breath as she felt the boards sinking under her feet. Walking carefully, she approached the front door. She studied it, a large decorative window in the heavy wood. She could hear Cleary moving around the porch, muttering to himself. She gave a small smile. She just knew Cleary from seeing him at church. He was new to the town, moving there in the last few years. Cavanagh felt somewhat safer with him there. She didn't think that anyone would challenge him.

Cleary stood next to Cavanagh, his head tilting to study her and then the door. He reached for the latch, finding the door opening under his hand. He had sort of expected that but was still surprised.

"Are you going in?" Cleary waited for Cavanagh to respond. "And just for the record, you're not going in on your own." His voice and face were stern. There was no way that he would let a lady go into an abandoned house on her own.

Cavanagh nodded, pausing to study the door and the lock. This is strange, she thought. This has been open for a long time. It was an old-fashioned lock that needed an old-fashioned key. She had skeleton keys in her kit in the van. She would retrieve them shortly.

Cleary stepped further into the house, a breath drawn in sharply as the floor creaked and seem to sag under his steps. His hand went out to prevent Cavanagh from moving forward.

"This isn't safe, Cavanagh. The floor is too weak for us to walk on." Cleary's head dropped as Cavanagh stepped around him and stopped five feet from him.

"I need to see the other doors, Cleary, to assess what I need to do." She looked around. "This place has been empty for at least twenty years. It's the local ghost house."

"I can see that." He stepped carefully towards her.

A sudden snap caused his heart to stutter. He leapt towards Cavanagh, wrapping her into his arms and throwing them sideways towards safety. They just didn't reach it. The flooring gave way, opening up a cavity to the cellar. A scream was torn from Cavanagh as they fell through to the dirt floor and then were still.

The men who had approached the house shared a gleeful look. This is what they had hoped would happen. They stood at the open front door and stared at the cavity. Turning, they looked at the vans and then at one another. Two of the men ran for the vans and drove away with them.

The tall and lean man garbed in black clothes continued to stare at the hole in the floor before a maniacal laugh emanated from him. He turned and walked away, seeming to match the dark bare branches of the deciduous trees.

Dust and debris floated through the air to settle on the couple. Neither moved, the fall being more devastating than the men had planned. Only God knew where they were. Their disappearance would cause great consternation in Cavanagh's family but not in Cleary's. He was an orphan.

Chapter 2

The next morning, Foley stood in the work shop at the locksmith's business. He frowned. Cavanagh was not there. He had driven by her home on his way in and her van had been parked in the driveway as was her personal truck. This was not like her not to be the first one in to work.

"Dad? Have you seen Cavanagh?" Foley turned as he heard his father entering the shop.

"Cavanagh? No, I haven't." Dagen frowned at his son. "Isn't she here?"

"No, she's not. That's not like her. In fact, I haven't heard from her since around noon yesterday." The two men stared at one another before Dagen reached to pull his son from the shop and locked the door.

The father and grandfather walked rapidly up to the work van parked in Cavanagh's driveway. Foley reached to tug at the door handle. It was locked just as he suspected that it would be. He peered over at Dagen as he shrugged, having tried her truck doors and found them locked.

Foley reached for his keys, unlocking the front door and deactivating the security system. He walked through his daughter's single story home and through the basement without finding her. He frowned. This was not like her. She was careful not to worry him too much, especially when it came to work duties. Foley turned as he heard a sound from his father.

"Dad?" He looked towards his father, finding Dagen rising to an upright position once more. "What do you have?"

"Cavanagh's keys. I suspect that they were shoved through the mail slot. This is not good, son. She would not have done that." His keen eyes in his lined and aged face studied his son, worried about both his son and his granddaughter.

"Her keys?" Foley stopped himself for taking them. "No, she would not have done that. We need to call it in. Do we know where she was heading yesterday?"

"No, I don't know that we do. We'll need to check the logs at work." Dagen reached for his phone. Cavanagh was an adult and able to move around without their presence or consent. But this was totally out of character for her. Given their line of work, they needed to find her and find her fast.

Back at their work place, Foley searched through the order book and then the work emails. He sat back as he read the one that had sent his daughter out on a job.

"Here, Dad. She went out to the Lockyer place. I wouldn't this place would need any locks changed. It's been deserted for years." He looked up, fear for his daughter on his face.

"That is strange, son." Dagen reached for the phone, intent in calling for help. He calmly explained to the emergency services dispatcher what they knew. Cavanagh was well known in her town for helping people. Had this care and compassion of hers harmed her? Dagen was afraid for his beloved and only grandchild. She had been missing for close to a ay and that was unacceptable.

A patrol officer stepped from his vehicle at the Lockyer house and stared around. He could see the tire tracks that had crushed the overgrown driveway. Two separate vehicles, he decided, before he walked around the house. He eyed the porch and stepped cautiously upon it. The front door was locked, he discovered, as were all the other doors.

Bob stepped back from the house to lean against his vehicle. His arms crossed over his chest, he studied the building and then the footprints that he could see even though it was hours since someone had been there. More than one person, he thought, although two sets of footprints didn't return from the building. His head turned as he heard another vehicle.

George stepped from his patrol SUV before he too studied the building as well. His feet took him to where Bob stood. They were friends of Cavanagh and didn't understand her not being in touch with her father or grandfather and definitely not turning up for work that morning.

"Bob? Any sign of her?"

Bob sighed. He had to go into that building. Only he didn't want to. He knew that it was in rough shape and could collapse at any time.

"I tried the doors and they're locked." Bob frowned. "At least, I think that they were." He nodded at the overgrown front path. "People have been in here and two people didn't come back unless they were carried."

George's hands clenched where he had them on his police vest. The two men share a look before they were walking rapidly towards the house. Their steps were cautious as they approached the front door, feeling the planks swaying under their feet. Bob's hand hesitated for a moment before he reached for the door latch. He looked sideways at James as this time the latch moved under his hand and the door creaked slowly open.

"This was locked, George." He was shocked to say the least.

George stared at him and then at the partially open door. He had no doubt that Bob was correct. He peered into the dimness of the house, brushing away spider webs as he did so. The wide beam from his flashlight illuminate the room before his gaze dropped.

"The floor's given way, Bob. And it looks fresh."

The two officers exchanged glances before George's hand was tight in Bob's before he leaned forward to peer into the hole. His light flashed around the crevice before something caught his eye. His light returned to that area and he drew in a deep breath before he was stepping back.

"She's down there, Bob. And so is a man. I wonder who." George was off the porch and running for his car to call for emergency services.

Bob stared with horror towards the hole. This was not what he had expected to find. He prayed for his friend and whoever it was that was done there as well. He knew that they needed help and needed help quickly. Only the conditions meant that the emergency services who responded would need to move slowly and carefully.

George was back beside Bob, his hands clenching and unclenching. He too was a friend of Cavanagh's. Who had done this was a question that ran through both men's minds.

Chapter 3

The rumble of heavy vehicles disturbed the peace of the area and caused the critters and birds to flee. The fire rig stopped behind the patrol vehicles before men dropped down to the ground. The paramedic rig stopped as well before the paramedics were running towards the two officers.

"What do we have?" The fire captain approached Bob, eyeing him and then the house.

"Cavanagh. She's fallen through the floor. The floor gave way, I suspect, and she dropped to the basement. There's a man with her as well."

The fire captain stared at Bob and then the house once more.

"I heard that Cleary O'Shea didn't turn up for a job this morning. Is that him down there?"

Bob shrugged. He had no idea. He was not that familiar with Cleary so he couldn't say or sure if it was him. He watched as the firefighters moved towards the house and cautiously approached the door. The scene then began busy, with equipment brought in to lower the paramedics to the basement as well as a couple of firefighters. He reached into his vehicle for his radio, knowing that they needed an investigator and a crime scene team on site.

The paramedics reached carefully to assess the two in the basement. They were alive but in grave condition, the team decided. They worked to move them carefully to backboards. Cavanagh gave a whimper of pain as her back landed on the backboard, a neck collar in place. She was strapped to the board before the back board was lifted and then carefully raised to waiting hands.

The men looked around the cellar as they worked, their eyes rising to the hole above them. The couple had fallen about nine feet. They shared more than one look as they worked to brush away the dust, debris, and bits of wood that lay on top on them. At some point, they decided that Cleary must have roused enough to move closer to Cavanagh in an attempt to keep her warm from the dampness and chill that was present in the cellar.

Cleary didn't move or stir at all as the motions were repeated with him. His breathing was shallow and the men feared that he had devastating internal injuries. Rushed from the building once he was lifted up to waiting hands, his backboard was placed into the paramedic rig. A firefighter jumped behind the wheel as both paramedics climbed into the back to work on the two, the door slamming shut behind them.

Foley and Dagen ran for the waiting room and then the clerk, fear on their faces. James had appeared at their locksmith shop, simply stating that Cavanagh had been found but was hurt. He didn't give any details and neither man had asked for that.

Foley paced the waiting room, sure that his daughter was dead. He had raised her after her mother had died in childbirth. The father and daughter had a close bond. His parents had been instrumental in helping in her early years before his mother had died from a heart attack just as Cavanagh was reaching her teens. That had not stopped her grandfather from stepping in.

"Son, sit." Dagen reached an arm out to wrap around his son's shoulders. "Sit and we'll pray. I called for Matthew to come." Matthew was their pastor and a good friend of Foley's. "He'll be here shortly."

Slumping on a chair, Foley finally nodded at his father's words.

"Thanks, Dad. I should have called." His eyes were on the door behind where his daughter was. "Did I hear rightly?"

"What was that?" Dagen wasn't sure if he had heard anything other than that Cavanagh was found but hurt.

"Did James say that a man had been found as well?" Foley turned as he felt someone sit near him. James had approached in time to hear Foley's question.

"You did. A Cleary O'Shea."

"Cleary? What was he doing there?" Dagen knew the younger man, having taken him under his wing so to say after meeting him at church. He didn't think that his family was aware of that.

"Cleary. He's a surveyor, isn't he?" James shared a look with Dagen.

"He is. Don't tell me that he was called out there as well." Dagen sat back, shock on his face before he was on his feet, heading for the clerk. He wanted to ensure that he was down as next of kin for Cleary. Cleary was an orphan and had no one who could step in. He returned to sit beside his son, confident that he could and would step in for Cleary.

Hearing his name called out, Dagen rose once more and headed for the nurse. She gave him a small smile and then pointed towards a cubicle.

"In there, Dagen. The surgeon needs to speak with you."

Dagen hesitated, a prayer rising for his young friend, before he shoved the curtain aside enough to enter. He hesitated once more before he approached the stretcher, not liking the fact that Cleary was not moving.

The surgeon eyed Dagen and nodded at him. He had been told that Dagen had stepped in for Cleary.

"Dagen?" His voice caused Dagen to jump.

"Gerry? How is he?"

"Not great, Dagen. He has some injuries including a broken leg from his fall. He also has been out there all night, causing some hypothermia. We'll treat the injuries but he won't be going home for a few days. I just need to go over the treatment options with you and then have you sign the consents that we need you to."

Dagen nodded as he listened to Gerry. The surgeon was correct. Cleary would not be going home that day. And Dagen was determined that Cleary stay with him when he was first released. He turned and walked out of the room, finding a nurse waiting for him. Her hand on his arm directed him towards another cubicle. He could hear Foley's voice and sighed. He didn't want to know the injuries that his granddaughter had suffered but he would. He would not walk away from either her or Foley, not when they both needed him.

Foley stood at his daughter's side, fear and worry evident on his face. He had been called back shortly after Dagen had disappeared to find Cleary. He watched his daughter's face, hearing the faint whimpers of pain as she moved restlessly. The physician was on his way in, he was told, and would give him all the details of his daughter's injuries. Foley didn't like the sound of that.

The physician, a stranger to their town, paused as he studied Foley. He didn't like that this young lady had been hurt.

"Mr. O'Rourke? Let me explain what we have found with your daughter." The physician detailed her injuries before stating that she would need time to recover. She had torn ligaments in her shoulder but those would heal on their own. She just couldn't use that arm for weeks. And Cavanagh had a concussion, which had been expected.

"God was there, Doctor." Foley didn't look at the man to see the sneer that crossed the man's face.

Dagen saw it as he stopped at his son's side. His stern glance caught the physician's attention who shrugged and walked away. His arm was around his son and his other hand rested on his granddaughter's arm. God was the Great Physician and would heal both the young people, with his help of course. Somehow, Dagen had determined to find the keys that would unlock the mystery of what had happened and open the door to solve it.

Chapter 4

Cavanagh roused enough to hear her father's voice but not enough to respond. Her shoulder hurt, she decided, not knowing what she had done to it. She tried to pull the sling from it, only to have a hand on hers and stop it. A whimper of pain escaped for her before she slept. The pain medications were working and she didn't hear the soft voices of the two men in her life who were extremely worried about her.

Foley prayed for healing for his daughter. He didn't understand why she had been at that mansion. It had been abandoned for so many years that there would be no need for a locksmith. Foley frowned as he remembers the words asking, no demanding, that Cavanagh come on her own. It was a set-up, he decided, and he wanted to know who it was who had wished to harm his beloved daughter.

Dagen had walked away, anger on his face. This was puzzling to him but he was still angered by the events. He paused for a moment before he shook his head covered in thick gray waves. Dagen headed for Cleary, thoroughly worried about the younger man. He had yet to rouse, even though he had been through surgery and was now in a hospital room.

Bob walked towards Dagen, a hand out to stop the man that all of Cavanagh's friends thought of as another grandfather. He took time for each one of the friends, just as Cavanagh did.

"Dagen? How are they?" Bob kept his hand on Dagen's arm, balancing a tray of take-out coffees in his other hand.

"Cavanagh roused somewhat." Dagen sighed. "She has damaged her shoulder and that will take time to heal. She'll be facing physiotherapy after that." He paused, working to control his emotions. "Cleary has had to have his leg set. He broke his femur. That puts him out of work for a while."

"It will." Bob release Dagen's arm before he pointed at the waiting room. "Come and sit for a while. I have a coffee here for you and Foley. Let me give him his and then we'll sit for a while. We need to pray for these two."

Dagen found a seat and then closed his eyes. It was early evening already and he was exhausted. The worry for his granddaughter had been immense. His world revolved around Cavanagh and Foley and it seemed to have expanded to include Cleary.

Bob sat quietly. He was off duty and had changed into street clothes. He had no intention of leaving the two older men on their own. Bob knew that James was heading their way as were a number of other officers.

"Bob? Who's the investigator?" Foley sat nearby, his cup of coffee clutched in his hand.

"The investigator? It's Will Passmore. He'll be around tonight, he said." Bob studied Foley, seeing the strain that he was trying hard to hide. "He's working the scene still, he said."

"Okay. That works." Foley was friends with Will and knew how he would keep his promise to be there. He watched the activity around him before his eyes closed. He wasn't sleeping. Foley was praying for everyone involved and in particular his daughter.

Will paused before he entered the hospital. He was frustrated. There was no reason for the accident that had happened. Only, he was not convinced that it was an accident. The techs were still working through what they had gathered. He turned as he heard footsteps beside him and wrapped his wife in his arms. Amy had come to find him, knowing how hard the force was taking what had happened. Cavanagh and her family were huge supporters of the force.

"Will? How is she?" Amy was almost afraid to ask.

"I'm not sure at the moment. I haven't had a chance to speak with either Dagen or Foley." His hand reached for his wife's. Cavanagh was a friend of Amy's and what had happened disturbed and worried both of them.

Will waited as Amy greeted Foley and Dagen before he moved in on the two men. Dagen studied the detective, getting a sense that Will didn't have a lot of good news for them.

"Will?" Dagen nodded his head towards the hallway. "Let's walk."

Will agreed. He needed speak with Dagen but he wasn't sure how to proceed.

"Talk to me, Will. You never have a problem doing that. What can you tell me?"

Will shrugged. He wasn't sure what to say.

"They were found in the cellar, Dagen. I think that you know that. The floor gave way under them." Will turned to study the waiting room, seeing Foley watching him closely.

"I wish that I had known that she was missing and there. They're treating both of them for mild hypothermia." Dagen was troubled to say the least.

"We didn't. She's independent, Dagen, and you would not change that about her. She has never been in trouble. Her heart is good and God has used her in ways that we don't see."

"She does." Dagen rubbed at his cheek, worried about his beloved granddaughter. "How do we find out who it was?"

"That's where we come in. We're working on it but it is still early. Do you know why she was here?" Will's notebook was out.

"She had an email asking that she come out there. That there were locks to change. And she was to come on her own." Dagen was greatly troubled by that.

"She was? That's unusual?" Will wasn't sure about that, not quite sure how the locksmith business worked.

"It is. We usually go out on our own. It's just not that we are asked to come on our own." Dagen felt Foley's hand on his shoulder.

"I see. I'll need copies of those, if I can. I'll arrange for a warrant just to be on the legal side." Will walked away at last. Amy had elected to stay with the two men.

Dagen turned to his son before he wrapped him into a hug. They had had enough tragedy in their lives. They didn't need to worry about Cavanagh.

"Let's go see our girl, son." Dagen turned Foley towards Cavanagh's room, praying that she would be awake but knowing that was unlikely. Neither one of them planned to leave that night. They were both adamant about that.

Dagen walked away after an hour, heading for Cleary. He stood at the young man's bedside, studying the bruising on his face and then the blankets that were arched above the leg. He prayed for Cleary, knowing that Cleary faced an uphill battle in his recovery. Dagen just didn't understand the why's of what had happened. He wasn't sure that he ever would.

Foley's head was bowed as he sat beside Cavanagh's bedside. She was restless as she slept. The physician had been around and stated that was normal. He would be back in the morning.

His head was raised as he sensed someone nearby. There was no one who he could see. He sighed. God was there and had let Foley know that he was not on his own. This is what Foley had experienced in the past. He just didn't expect to experience that while in a hospital room with his daughter.

Amy walked back through the hallways, searching for the two men. She simply stood with an arm around them and prayed for each one and for her friend, Cavanagh. She didn't know Cleary but suspected that would change.

Chapter 5

Cavanagh's head stilled its restless motions as she roused. She cracked open her eyes, uncertain as to why she was hurting so badly. A hand reached for the sling even as she frowned. Cavanagh had no idea what she had done. She couldn't remember anything past the previous weekend when she had escaped for a few days and found a small cabin to hide in.

She sensed someone near her and cautiously peeked that way. Dagen stood there, his hands clasped tightly around the steel bed rail. His eyes were closed and Cavanagh knew that he was praying for his granddaughter. Her hand reached to touch his and then his covered hers.

Dagen looked at his granddaughter, taking in the dark shadows that lined her face under her eyes and the lines of pain that covered her face as well.

"Cavanagh?" Dagen's voice was kept low, just because of where he was. He was deeply worried about Cavanagh.

"Grand? What happened? Why am I here?" Cavanagh was beginning to panic, an unusual circumstance for her.

"You were hurt two days ago, love. You went to the Lockyer house on a request. Do you remember that?"

Cavanagh frowned at him. She wasn't certain that she had heard him correctly.

"The Lockyer house? Why would I go there? It's abandoned and ready to fall down." Her eyes slid closed for a moment. "What happened, Grand?"

"You were inside the house. The floor gave way under you. It was the next day before we knew that you were missing. We tracked through the emails at work and tracked you down. Bob and George found you." Dagen hesitated for a moment. "You've damaged some tendons. You'll not be working for a while."

Cavanagh sighed. She didn't need this, she decided. *God, I know that You are here. Why did this happen?*

"There is something else, Cavanagh. You were not alone." Dagen watched as Cavanagh's eyes slid closed and then popped open.

"I wasn't? Who was there?" Cavanagh waited for her grandfather to speak, knowing that it would take some time to get the words out. "Grand? Who was there?"

"Cleary O'Shea. He was called out there as well for a work project. He went down into the cellar as well."

"Cleary? I don't know him other than for knowing him from church. What happened, Grand? Why me? Who would do this?" Cavanagh's head went back against the pillows. Tears of pain, worry, and fear tricked down her face. She had never been a lady who wept. Today? Today, she could not stop the tears, causing great consternation in her grandfather.

Foley stood just outside the doorway, listening to the conversation between his father and his daughter. He was filled with worry and fear as well. No one could tell him why or who. And if they couldn't do that, then Cavanagh was still in grave danger. All he could do was petition heaven for protection for his beloved little girl. Foley turned away and walked the few feet down the hallway to Cleary's room. He had been in and out of it over the course of the night, waiting somewhat impatiently for Cleary to rouse. That had not happened to that point in time.

Dawn was beginning to lighten the sullen sky to the east as Cleary began to finally rouse and move. A hand reached for his leg, the pain driving through the darkness that he was in and bringing him the surface of awareness. He began to rouse more and more, his body twisting with pain before a hand on his shoulders stopped his movements.

Foley had approached the bed, watching as the younger man was struggling to rouse. He felt he had no option but to try and still Cleary's movements with a hand to his shoulder. All he could do for Cleary was do what he did for his daughter and that was to pray fervently for him.

Cleary's eyes finally opened and stayed open. He searched the room, certain that someone was there and after him. Only, he had no idea why or who. His gaze raised and stopped as he found Foley by his bedside, his head bowed in prayer. Clearing his throat, Cleary tried to speak. It took multiple attempts with his dry mouth and throat to even speak in a whisper.

"What happened? Where am I? And who are you?" Cleary's eyes didn't leave the man beside him. He was sure that he knew him but he wasn't sure about that. Nothing was making sense at the present time.

Foley looked up, taking in the equipment and furnishings in the hospital room. He looked down at Cleary, knowing that he had to speak and not sure what to say.

"I'm Foley O'Rourke. I understand that my father, Dagen, is a friend of yours. You're in our local hospital. You were injured at the same time as my daughter, Cavanagh. Why were you at the Lockyer house?"

"The Lockyer house? I don't know that I am familiar with that place. Should I know it?" Cleary raised the head of the bed, grimacing with pain as he did so. "What did I do?"

"Broke your femur and suffered mild hypothermia. The investigator wants to speak with you and should be around soon. Just so you know? My daughter, Cavanagh, was there as well and went through the floor with you. It was almost twenty-four hours before you were found." Frustrated, Foley turned and walked away. He didn't turn as he heard Cleary asking more questions and then asking for Foley to return.

Cleary's head went back on the pillow, his eyes closing. He attempted to pray but felt that his prayers were not rising any higher than the bed he was laying on. He sighed before he slept once more. He didn't hear Dagen approaching him and then walking away.

Will faced Foley just outside Cleary's room before he looked past the older man. He sighed to himself. He did need to speak with Cleary but from the look on Foley's face, he wasn't sure that he would be able to.

"Foley?" Will winced as his voice sounded loud in the early morning hush in the hospital.

"He's been awake, Will. He doesn't remember being there and he doesn't remember Cavanagh being there. Do you have any answers yet?" Foley didn't wait for an answer. He walked away, his shoulders slumping under the burden he was bearing.

Will watched him walk away. All he could do at present was to pray for his friends. There had not been one bit of evidence that explained away what had happened. He wanted to solve it and solve it yesterday. He lifted his eyes towards the ceiling, begging God for the key that would unlock this mystery before his hand shoved at the room door and he disappeared into Cleary's room.

Chapter 6

That afternoon, Cleary stared glumly at the large cast that covered most of his left leg. This was not good, he decided. He had to work. He had surveys pending and on the books that he had to get to. Cleary stared around the hospital room before he slid to the side of the bed and then sat, waiting until his head to clear. He reached for the crutches and then thumped his way to a cupboard, finding clothes waiting for him. Dagen had been around not that long before, pointing to the cupboard.

Dressing with a great deal of difficulty, Cleary slumped against a wall. That simple and familiar act had strained his strength and weakened him. He sighed. This is not what he wanted but it seemed to be what he had. He prayed for healing quickly and then opened the bathroom door to find Dagen waiting for him.

"Cleary? You're coming home with me for a couple of days. No arguments. It's either that or I in move with you." Dagen reached to steady Cleary. "I have your discharge papers and also your wheelchair."

Cleary nodded, his vision blurry for a moment. There was no way that he could manage on his own for the next couple of days. He sat in the wheelchair, waiting to be pushed towards the elevators.

Dagen stopped beside Cavanagh, reaching to carefully hug his granddaughter.

"All set, love?"

Dagen's question brought Cleary's head around to stare at the beautiful lady his age who stood there. His mouth opened and then snapped closed.

"This is my granddaughter, Cavanagh, Cleary. You two are sharing an adventure that we want over yesterday." Dagen's voice was stern.

"Grand? Take it easy on him. It's not his fault." Cavanagh's brow wrinkled for a moment. "At least, I don't think that it is." Cavanagh walked away at that, heading to punch at the button for the elevator. She was frustrated and hurting. Those two emotions were not ones that she dealt with easily.

"Dagen?" Cleary shifted to peer up at the older man. "What did she mean?"

"She means that we have no idea why you two were out there or why this happened. I'm not convinced that the floor just gave out like that." Dagen shoved at the wheelchair, heading to where Cavanagh was waiting and holding the elevator door for them. "Cavanagh? Your dad grabbed your stuff?"

"He did. I don't like this, Grand. I want to go home." Cavanagh was disgruntled and showed it, knowing that her grandfather would take it as she meant it and that it was not aimed at him.

"We know that you don't, love. Just stay with me for a couple of days and then you can head home. It was only two days since you were found." Dagen rubbed at his forehead, knowing that once Cavanagh was feeling more like herself, she would be off on her own and likely trying to work.

Cavanagh sighed, knowing that her grandfather was correct. She focused on Cleary from where she stood off to his side, a frown on her face. She had no idea why he had been there. She could remember speaking with him before the floor collapsed. Cavanagh had relived that collapse over and over in her dreams.

Settled onto a couch in Dagen's living room, Cleary's eyes closed. The pain was coming in waves. He had broken bones before but not like this. His body felt battered and bruised from the fall. Cleary had glimpses of the floor collapsing and him reaching for Cavanagh. He just didn't know if he had reached her in time to help save her from harm and he would not ask if he had.

Cavanagh worked away in the kitchen as best that she could with one hand. She was praising God that it was not her dominant hand that restricted but she still was working short-handed as she called it. Dagen worked away beside her, preparing a light supper for them all. He turned as he heard voices and nodded. Foley had appeared as had Will. It was expected that Foley would be here where his daughter was. And it was also expected that Will would show up to speak with the two younger people.

Foley reached to carefully hug his daughter before he took the tray of food from in front of her. Cavanagh had been contemplating how to pick it up without hurting. Her father had solved that mystery for her.

"Cavanagh?" Foley didn't ask the question that hovered at the end of his tongue.

"I'm okay, Dad, for now. I hurt and I know that I can't work for a while." She sighed. "I guess that I'm in the office."

"For now. We'll assess what we do as we go along. You need to heal, love, in more ways than one. Sari has asked if she can come and speak with you." Sari was a friend of Dagen's who had worked as a counsellor before she retired.

Cavanagh shrugged. She wasn't sure what that would accomplish but she was open to that.

"I guess, Dad. I'm not sure what that will solve."

"We'll work through it. Your grandfather and I will speak with you. Now, let's eat. Then, we spend time in prayer." Foley walked away, leaving Will standing near to Cavanagh.

"Cavanagh?" Will's voice was quiet. "How are you really doing?"

Cavanagh shrugged once more. She really didn't know how she felt. She was deeply afraid without knowing why and she was afraid for her father and grandfather. And yes, she was afraid for Cleary.

"I don't know how to feel, Will. I'm hurting. I can't do my work. I'm worried about the guys in my life who are worried about me. And now I have someone else to worry about." Cavanagh glared at him as he continued to grin. "This is not funny, buster."

"I know, Cavanagh. I do know that. Your response is just so you."

Cavanagh snorted. She and Will had been friends for too long for either one of them to really hide their feelings from one another.

"I don't understand, Will. Why was I out there? That building is too decrepit to need locks changed on it."

"We know that, Cavanagh. It's something that we're trying to work through. The email that you received? The email address where it was sent from no longer exists." Will was troubled by that.

"That's par for the course." Cavanagh moved to where she could watch Cleary. "What's the story with Cleary?"

"He was asked to survey the property. It seems that he found you instead. Thankfully he did. You were close enough when you were unconscious so that you were able to somewhat help keep each other warm. Cleary said that he remembers moving at some point closer to you. Only he's not clear on that." Will's hand went up as Cavanagh's mouth popped out. "And before you ask, we have the email that arranged it all. It was the same email address as yours."

"Well, that's no help." Cavanagh's matter-of-fact response was just so her that Will had to laugh, bringing Cleary's attention to Cavanagh.

Chapter 8

Cleary watched Cavanagh as she stood beside Will as they spoke. He suddenly wished that he was the one standing and speaking with her instead of Will. He shifted on his seat, causing Dagen to study the younger man before the older man nodded. Dagen could see that Cleary was trying hard to hide his interest in Cavanagh.

Cavanagh finally moved away from Will, heading for the couch and dropping to a sitting position beside Cleary. She sent him a sidelong look before she sighed to herself. She was hurting, she decided, and working with only one hand was cumbersome and difficult.

Cleary reached for her plate of food and waited until she took it before he took his own. He stared at the sandwich, not sure that he wanted to eat but needed to.

"Cavanagh? May I call you that?" Cleary kept his voice low under the level of the conversation around them.

"You can. It seems as if we are connected through this. I just don't understand it." Cavanagh was sober and angry. She didn't need this, she decided, but it seems as if God had decided that she needed to slow down. She just wished that He had chosen a different route.

"I don't either. I don't remember much of what happened other than driving into that laneway. What can you tell me?" Cleary was hopeful that Cavanagh would be able to tell him enough to unlock the door to his memory.

"I can't tell you much. You drove up, we introduced ourselves, and then we walked in the front door. We walked forward a few steps as I wanted to look at the doors from the inside. Then the floor just gave way under us. I can remember screaming but not much more than that. I gather that you're not remembering a lot."

"No, I'm not. I don't understand about that house. Will and Dagen both tell me that it is pretty much collapsing." Cleary rubbed at the cast on his leg. "I could see why I would be there but not you."

"That's what is so puzzling about it all. I shouldn't have been there. The locks should not have needed to be changed. After all the windows were all broken. A lock on the door would not keep anyone out. I just don't understand." Cavanagh lifted her sandwich and bit into it, not really paying attention to what she was doing.

"It is strange, Cavanagh. We'll need to work together on this to solve it." Cleary began to eat, oblivious to the startled stare that Cavanagh had fixed on him.

Neither one of them saw Foley watching them. They also didn't know that he had heard their conversation. That conversation worried him. He just knew that his daughter would not sit back and let Will and his fellow investigators determine what had happened to them. Foley drew in a deep breath. He was suddenly deeply afraid for his daughter and this young man. God had brought them together. It was up to them, he felt, to keep them safe. Foley could hear Cavanagh's voice telling him that he was doing God's job for Him and that he needed to stop.

Will walked away later. He too was deeply worried about his friend and his new acquaintance. He was only too well aware of how much danger these two could be in. He didn't like that it was hitting so close to home, as it was put.

Cavanagh walked away from the men in her life, which number now seemed to include Cleary. She was not too sure how she felt about that. Cavanagh shut the bedroom door quietly behind her before she turned to study the room which had been hers as a child and teen. She had not expected to be back there, not like this.

Cleary thumped his way to the bedroom on the first floor that he had been told to use. He slid to a sitting position on the side of the bed. He was tired and knew that he would not be keeping his eyes open for long. He could only pray for his friend and her father and grandfather. He petitioned heaven for protection for them as well as a swift resolution to the mystery.

Two days later found Cavanagh in the locksmith's shop, facing her father across the counter at the entrance. She was there to work. Only he was telling her that she couldn't. Cavanagh was growing angry, not at her father but at the circumstances that she found herself in. She disliked working in the shop and would rather be out on job sites. That wouldn't happen for a few weeks, she was told.

"Dad? What am I to do then?" Cavanagh was frustrated at her father's edict that she could not be out and about working at changing locks.

"I know, love. I know. You don't like this. But you do have to heal. And you can't do that if you keep using that arm." Foley was equally frustrated. He heard a soft snicker from behind him. "Thanks, Dad."

Dagen laid an arm across his son's shoulders, his eyes on his granddaughter.

"None of us like these circumstances, Foley and Cavanagh. We don't know who did this, Cavanagh. That means that you are at risk. And when you are finally able to be out and changing locks, you could put someone at risk just because."

Cavanagh finally nodded her agreement with her grandfather. She had tried to think through who it could have been and just couldn't come up with a name. Will had asked her that the day before and she had simply shrugged.

"I know, Grand. I do know that. But what do I do?" Cavanagh wrapped her arms around herself and then walked away.

Foley and Dagen watched her as did Cleary who had simply nodded in agreement when Foley asked him to come to their shop that morning. The plan was for Dagen then to take Cleary to his office.

"Cleary? What can Cavanagh do for you?" Dagen turned to the younger man, a frown on his face as he saw the look that Cleary had on his face. His gaze turned towards his granddaughter, finding Cavanagh watching Cleary in return.

Cleary shrugged. He wasn't sure what she could do for him. He was not even sure what he could do himself.

"I would have to see. I need to look at what I have on the books to see what I can put off." Cleary was frustrated as well. This was the busy season for him and he could not afford to lose clients by being laid up. His eyes rested thoughtfully on Cavanagh. Just maybe, he decided, he could use her help.

"How be we head over there in a while, Cleary?" Dagen walked to hug his granddaughter before moving past her towards the board that held their orders. He frowned at it for a moment before he begged God to protect the young couple. He turned a thoughtful look towards the front of the shop before he nodded. God was at work, he knew. He just wished that he knew what the plans were.

Chapter 9

That afternoon, Cleary turned from his desk, his leg aching. He was exhausted and should be heading home. Only he didn't want to. If he did go home, Cavanagh would not be there. Cleary wanted to be where Cavanagh was. He watched as she moved restlessly around the office and his shop, a frown on his face. He didn't know what to think. He only wanted to ensure that she was safe and that wasn't possible at the moment.

Dagen watched the two younger people, a half-smile on his face. The couple were dancing around one another, not wanting to look at one another. Their conversation was brief when they did speak. He decided that he needed to step in and straighten them out.

"Cavanagh? What are your plans?" Dagen waited patiently for Cavanagh to speak.

Cavanagh shrugged. She had no idea what she was going to do. Her gaze landed on Cleary who was watching her in return.

"I don't know, Grand. I can work in the shop but that's what you and Dad do. You're going to have to pick up the outside work. But what about Cleary? He can't do his work."

Cleary shook his head. He could still do most of what he did. There were certain aspects that he couldn't. He just wanted to know who had done this to them, tricked them into coming to that house and then setting them up to go through the floor. Cleary had asked Will just that. Will had not had an answer for him. Nor did Foley or Dagen. He still wanted to speak with Cavanagh. Cleary just wasn't sure how to do that.

"I have a suggestion, Cavanagh. You still have the ability to walk. You could work with Cleary and help out where he needs it. That way you two would be together. It would be easier to watch out for you two."

Cavanagh stared at her grandfather, not looking to where Cleary leaned on his crutches. She was exhausted and in pain and certainly didn't want her family planning her life for her. She sighed. Dagen meant well. She just didn't want to do that. The vibrating of her phone caught her attention before she pulled it from her pocket and studied the message that she had just received. Will wanted to know where she was and if she was safe? He didn't say why but Cavanagh was suddenly and deeply afraid. This was out of character for her. But given what had happened, it was no wonder that Cavanagh felt this way.

Cleary was worried about his new friend. He didn't realize that Cavanagh was working her magic in his heart, wriggling her way in through the tiniest crack that had appeared. Cleary had been determined to remain single all of his life, not having had any family around him. He had been abandoned as a newborn and raised in the foster care system without anyone coming forward to adopt him.

"It could work, Cavanagh. We could always give it a try." Clearly frowned at her before a grin broke over his face.

Staring at him once more, Cavanagh couldn't believe what he had said. She turned away from him to stare out of a window. She vaguely heard Dagen leaving as she studied the parking lot of Cleary's building. She heard movement behind her and expected to hear him beside her. But he wasn't.

"Cleary? What do we know?" Cavanagh spoke quietly, hearing Cleary pausing as she spoke.

"Not a lot, I don't think, Cavanagh." Cleary leaned against a table in his work room, his eyes on his lady. "I haven't talked to Will today yet, but I am afraid for you. It seems as if this was directed at you."

Cavanagh was shaking her head. That wasn't correct, she decided.

"No, it affects both of us. I just don't know why." Cavanagh held up her phone. "Will sent me a text message, asking if I was safe." She shifted on her feet once more to watch Cleary in return. "Why is he asking that?"

"I don't know, Cavanagh. I'm not a police officer. But I imagine he has some sense or word or whatever that threatens you. And I would like to know why." Cleary's life had been hard and he had had to fight his way through life. His long-term foster parents had been dedicated Christians and raised him that way. It was life outside of their home that had challenged him too much.

Cleary turned away at that, his hands reading for his work orders. He sighed. There was no way that he could continue with them, at least not on his own. Dagen's suggestion would work, he knew. Other than that he would need to hire a labourer to work with him. He found his stool and sat, leaning his crutches against the table. Lost in thought, he didn't see Cavanagh watching him, a look on her face that showed that she was worried about him.

The front door flew open with a loud bang against the wall. Cavanagh jumped and screamed at four men rushed into the room. Two of the men headed her way and the other two Cleary's way. A hand grasped her wrist in a tight and cruel grip, pulling her towards the door. She fought with every bit of energy that she had. Her wrist was twisted and turned to try and free to no avail. Her long hair flew around her face, momentarily blinding her. Cavanagh tried to dig her feet into the flooring but the wooden flooring just didn't allow for that. She was pulled roughly from the building, hearing Cleary's shouts behind her for the men to let her go.

Cleary surged to his feet, forgetting for a moment that he couldn't weight bear on his left leg. The pain hit him hard and he staggered to try and regain his balance. That never happened. The other two men were on him and preventing him from reaching for his crutches. He hopped away, desperate to get out of the building and find Cavanagh.

Hard blows rained down on him, sending him to the floor. Kicks with work boots that contained steel toes hammered at his sides. He was left a further broken and bloodied form on the floor as the two men ran from the building and towards the truck that was waiting for them.

Cavanagh had been shoved into the back seat of the truck, the two men on either side of her. That didn't prevent her from struggling to escape, her good wrist still clamped in the man's hard grasp. A cloth over her mouth and nose had her struggling even more until her body went limp and she sagged back against the seat.

The men didn't talk as they sped away in the large black truck, intent on delivering Cavanagh to the house as they had been contracted to. She was pulled roughly from the truck, her limp body gathered up and roughly carried to a room in a house. Dumped on the bed, Cavanagh's left ankle was encased in a shackle before the men backed away and locked the door behind them. Cavanagh was not going anywhere.

Chapter 10

Dagen frowned as he walked towards Cleary's office. The front door was swinging open, not shut as it should be. He paused for a moment, knowing that Cavanagh or Cleary would have called him or Foley for a ride if they wanted to leave. And he had just been at the shop with Foley. Neither one of the men had heard from the couple.

His heart sinking, Dagen ran towards the shop, a hand out on the green steel door to shove it open further. He stepped inside, not seeing his granddaughter.

"Cavanagh? Cavanagh, are you here?" His voice echoed in the room. "Cleary? Are you around?" Dagen paced towards the work shop, his steps pausing once more as he stared in horror at Cleary. On his knees beside the younger man, Dagen reached with a hesitant and shaking hand to feel for a pulse.

Cleary was alive but badly hurt, Dagen could tell. On his feet once more, he searched for Cavanagh, not finding her anywhere. His phone was out as he dropped down beside Cleary once more.

"I need paramedics and police." Dagen's voice was shaking with his fear and worry. "At Cleary O'Shea's shop. He's been beaten. And Cavanagh is missing." He thanked the dispatcher before he stared at his phone. He punched in Foley's number in an almost violent manner. "Foley? I need you at Cleary's office. He's been hurt. Cavanagh is missing."

"What?" Foley's voice exploded. He ran for the car, the building door locked behind him. He sped towards Cleary's, praying that he didn't get pulled over for speeding. Once in the parking lot, he ran towards the building. Foley slid to a stop as a patrol officer held out a hand.

"I'm sorry, Foley. You need to stay out here." A sympathetic look was on the officer's face.

"Cavanagh?" Foley could barely find his breath to ask.

"I don't know, Foley. Your dad will be out in a few moments." He stepped to the side as the paramedics appeared, Cleary on the stretcher.

"Cleary?" Foley stepped closer and then walked beside the stretcher towards the paramedic rig.

"He's not responding, Foley." One of the paramedics spoke, his eyes on Foley. He knew that Cavanagh had disappeared and prayed for the young lady and her family. His gaze went back to Cleary before the stretcher was lifted into the back of the rig and the door shut, cutting off Foley's view of Cleary.

Dagen walked slowly towards his son, his feet as heavy as his heart. His beloved granddaughter was missing. Will was there and had taken over the investigation. He had shaken his head at the questioning look on Dagen's face. Dagen draped an arm around his son's shoulders.

Foley turned his head to study his father, seeing the devastation on his face.

"Dad?"

“I don’t know much. I’m not sure any of us do. I came back and found the door open. When I went inside, Cavanagh was missing and Cleary beaten. He hadn’t roused the whole time that I was with him or when they were working on him.”

“Where is she, Dad?” Foley blinked against the tears that clouded his vision. His daughter was missing once more. Only this time, he didn’t know where she might be. That worried and scared him.

“I don’t know, Foley. Will said he’d be out shortly to speak with us. Here. Have a seat at Cleary’s picnic table.” Dagen directed his son to the table and shoved him down. He in turn paced in short steps nearby, praying for the two young people and also praying for his son. Cavanagh was Foley’s whole world other than for his father.

Will stood just outside of the building, his eyes on the father and son. He sighed to himself. This is what he had been worried about early when he sent that text message to Cavanagh. He lifted his eyes to the sky, seeing that twilight was moving in. He feared for Cavanagh. There had not little to no evidence of what had happened to her. The crime scene techs had found scuff marks on the wooden floor that they assumed came from her shoes. There was also no evidence in the work room where Cleary had been beaten.

Foley looked up, a devastated look on his face. He was on his feet, walking swiftly towards Will.

“Will, what can you tell us?” Dagen once more had his arm around his son’s shoulders as Foley asked his question.

"I'm sorry, Foley, Dagen. There is not a lot of evidence. Cleary has security cameras but I can't access them without his consent or information." Will hesitated before he walked away, not sure how to proceed or what to say.

Foley stared after him. Will would have told him, they knew.

"Let's take your car to your place and then head for the hospital. Cleary needs someone there for him. I don't know that he has anyone."

"He doesn't, Dad. He told me that he was abandoned as a newborn and raised in foster care. That he moved here to get away from everything. He doesn't have a power of attorney for medical." Foley trudged to his car and slid into it. He hesitated before he drove off, his eyes on the building. Where was his daughter? Was she safe and alive?

Dagen approached the ward clerk at the entrance to the Emergency Department, having a quiet word with her. She nodded and then rose, heading back into the Department. She returned in a few moments and spoke just as quietly to Dagen. That man turned and found his son. He sat, his head bowing as he prayed for his granddaughter and then the young man who had become part of their lives.

"Dad?" Foley looked between his father and the clerk.

"I asked if we could be notified of Cleary's condition as he was a friend of ours and had no one else. They've agreed to that. It will be a while though.

He's not in great shape." Dagen's eyes closed once more as he fought his emotions.

"I don't understand, Dad. Why Cleary? And why Cavanagh? What is the reason for this?"

"I don't know, son. What I do know is that God is here with us and with Cavanagh. He is in control."

"I know that, Dad. It's just so hard to accept." Foley wiped at his eyes.

"It is hard, son. That's where our faith comes in. How be we spend our time waiting in prayer?" Dagen's head was bowed as he did just that.

Chapter 11

It was early morning before Cleary roused. He groaned, his groans sounding loud in the quiet and hushed hospital room. He cracked open his eyes, squinting around the room. He was in a hospital room once more. What was going on, Lord? He questioned why and how.

Foley was on his feet, reaching out a hand to rest it on Cleary's shoulder. That motion had Cleary looking up at Foley with a frown on his face.

"Do I know you?"

"You do, Cleary. I'm Foley, a friend of yours. How are you feeling?" Foley watched his young friend closely. He knew that Dagen was ensconced in the waiting room. Neither man had wanted to leave Cleary on his own.

"Horrible. What happened?" Cleary raised the head of the bed enough so that he was sitting upright somewhat.

"You were beaten yesterday and left in your work shop." Foley reached for his chair to pull it over so that he could sit. "Do you remember anything?"

Cleary shook his head and then regretted it. His head began to pound from the movement. He squinted at Foley who had grimaced at the pain that he saw on the younger man's face.

"Shouldn't have done that, Cleary." Foley gave a small swift grin.

“Thanks, I think. I don’t remember what happened? Do you know?” Cleary was desperate to find out why he was beaten.

“My daughter, Cavanagh, was at your office. She disappeared from it. We think that you were beaten to stop that. Unfortunately, you had already had a broken leg from the previous incident.”

“What are you talking about?” Cleary stared at Foley.

Foley proceeded then to tell him what had happened. Cleary stared at him in shock. This could not have happened. He was a surveyor, after all, and not involved in criminal activities.

Dagen approached the two men, not sure what had just transpired. A hand rested on his son’s shoulder as he studied Cleary. He winced at the colourful look on the younger man’s face.

“Cleary?”

“Dagen? What happened?” He knew that he was repeating his question. He trusted the man who had stepped in as a grandfather figure to him. Cleary didn’t know Foley and wasn’t sure how to react to him or whether he could trust his words. He prayed for peace about the situation, not sure what he was facing or even who Cavanagh was. “There has to be more to the story.”

“There is, son.” Dagen sighed and then prayed for the words that he needed. “Almost a week ago, I think it was, you were called to an old property to do a survey. For some reason, Cavanagh was called to the same property to change the locks. That wasn't necessary from what we can determine. You two went inside and the floor gave way. That's when you broke your femur. Cavanagh injured her shoulder. You were there for almost twenty-four hours when you were found. Now, yesterday, you were at your office. You were beaten to unconsciousness. God protected you and kept you alive. Cavanagh disappeared. We have no inkling of where she is." Dagen grew stern as he thought of her.

"I need out of here. I need to help you find her." Cleary tried to push off the sheet and light blanket but his eyes closed instead and he slept. He didn't hear the audible prayers that were offered for him.

"Dad?" Foley shifted his feet, turning partway to face his father. "Any word?"

"No, there isn't. Will was sent home to get some sleep. He'll be back in after ten, he said. He'll touch base with us then." Dagen was exhausted and frustrated. He wanted his granddaughter back home, but no one knew just where she was. And that was worrisome.

Foley finally nodded. His brain felt foggy, he decided. Lack of sleep and worry were draining his strength. He felt his father's hand turning him from the room and to a seat in the waiting room. Foley slept, not seeing that his father didn't but instead kept watch over his son.

Cleary was awake not that much later, pulling himself to a sitting position. He looked around before he shifted to the side of the bed and then swung his legs over the edge. Cleary waited for his head to clear before he reached for the nearby crutches and thumped around the room, finding his clothes and dressing before he headed from the room. He found Dagen and Foley and then a chair nearby. Dagen had dozed off as well, unable to prevent himself from that very deed.

Dozing off himself, Cleary didn't see the nurse who had come looking for him. She paused for a moment before she shook her head. Cleary should not be up and about. She also knew that nothing would keep him in that bed if he could be up. Foley and Dagen were still sleeping, the worry and terror for the young lady who they both loved driving through them even as they slept.

Will approached them, his steps quiet as he walked through the waiting room and found a seat. He studied each of the men and prayed for each one. He watched as Cleary roused, blinking as he cleared his vision.

"Cleary?" Will's voice was quiet in the stillness of the room.

Cleary jumped at Will's voice, turning to face Will. He frowned at Will before his face cleared.

"Will? Have you solved this yet?"

Will shook his head, a small grin briefly appearing on his face.

"Not yet, Cleary. But we do need to talk."

"If you want any information about yesterday, I don't know anything. I don't remember anything. I don't even remember Cavanagh, is it?"

“It is. You not remembering? It’s about what I expected.” Will had suspected that this would be the case. “Where are you heading?”

“To my home. I need to go there.” He looked at the two older men, finding that they were awake and listening to the conversation. “Until I remember, I am too dangerous to be around.”

“None of us think that, Cleary.” Dagen leaned forward, his elbows rested on his knees. “We know that you didn’t plan for this to happen. Let us help you.”

Chapter 12

Cleary thumped through his house on his crutches, finding the house stuffy and chilly. He had not been there for a few days. Dagen could be heard in the kitchen, putting away the groceries that Foley had obtained for the younger man. Foley had left, heading for Cavanagh's home, praying that his daughter would be there.

He headed for his bedroom, exhaustion hitting in waves. Setting aside the crutches, he sat on the bed and then stretched out. He knew that he needed to clean up but sleep was needed more at that time. Cleary didn't hear Dagen's footsteps as he searched for the younger man.

Dagen stood for a moment, studying his young friend, before he reached for a blanket and after shaking it out, he covered Cleary. He stood and prayed for him before he walked away. He reached for his mug of coffee and headed into the living room. There was no way that he was leaving Cleary on his own. Foley would be back to spend the night on watch for Cleary.

Will looked up from where he had seated himself, his laptop out in front of him. He had been making notes about this mystery, knowing that he had very little to work with. He sighed to himself and then prayed for wisdom in solving it. Will wanted it over and Cavanagh back with the men in her life

"Will? What can you tell me?" Dagen slumped into a chair, his emotions getting the better of him for a moment.

"There's not a lot that I can tell you, Dagen. We just don't have enough information to find Cavanagh. I wish that I could just walk in and bring her home." Will was upset by that but covered it up as best that he could.

"I gathered that, Will. I wish that it was over but it will take time, unfortunately." Dagen's eyes closed for a moment. He was exhausted, he had to admit.

It was hours later that Cleary roused, uncertain for a moment where he was. It was dark outside and his bedroom was lit by the bedside lamp. He frowned. He didn't remember turning it on.

On his feet or foot, rather, Cleary reached for clean clothes and showered as best he could before redressing and then thumping for the kitchen. He hesitated for a moment as he heard movement in there and then watched Foley preparing a meal for them.

Foley turned as he heard Cleary, watching his young friend. He was deeply troubled to say the least and not sure what to say or where to even be.

"Cleary? I'm sorry. I think I over-stepped in preparing a meal." Foley looked down at the sandwiches and the bowls of soup that he had set on the table.

"It's fine, Foley. It's okay. I shouldn't have slept." Cleary sank onto a chair, his eyes closing for a moment. His crutches were set to the side.

"You needed it." Foley sat as well and asked the blessing on their meal.

The two men ate in silence for a moment before Cleary rested his forearms on the table. He looked down at his bowl before he spoke.

"Do you know anything, Foley? Has Will said anything?" Cleary was praying that Will had solved this mystery and that Cavanagh was back home.

"He hasn't said anything. I don't think that he has enough information to solve it. At least, that's the impression that I'm getting." Foley was saddened at that.

"I see. What can we do to advance that investigation?" Cleary's head was clearing at last and he was beginning to see that somehow he and Cavanagh were in this adventure together. He just needed to find her.

"Dad and I were talking about that. We need to sit down, the three of us, and go through all the people who you know here. Cavanagh knows just about everyone here. We find the ones in common and look at them. Then we reach out further and further. I have friends who I can call on if we need to." Foley rubbed at his forehead. "I'm staying the night, Cleary. Dad will be in the shop in the morning and handle anything that we need. People are aware that Cavanagh is missing and are actively looking for her."

"Only they can't find her." Cleary thought through what little he knew. "It comes back to that house. What's the history of it?"

"The Lockyer house?" Foley sat back, a frown on his face. "Do you have paper and a pen, Cleary?"

Cleary nodded. He reached for his crutches, finding Foley's hand stopping him.

"If I may, just tell me where to find it. Your office?" At Cleary's nod, Foley was on his feet and headed that way. He returned with two pads of paper and pens. He sat once more, his eyes on Cleary. "Cleary, hear me out. We don't think that you are the cause of this. Will has not found anything that would cause us to think that. It seems to come back to that house. Cavanagh and you were lured that way. He has said that the floor was weak but should not have collapsed. He had someone in to take a look at it. The floor joists were weakened by someone and that's why it collapsed. This was planned. We just don't know who planned it."

"No, we don't. I'm not from this town. I was driving through it one day and just decided to stay. You didn't have a surveyor here. My work has picked up a lot since I set up my business. I don't know the history of this town." Cleary's pen tapped on the pad of paper. "What can you tell me?"

Foley nodded, turning as he heard a tap at the door and then Will appeared.

"Will?"

"I know. I'm here. I just wanted to see if Cleary had remembered anything."

Cleary was shaking his head.

"I haven't remembered much of anything, Will. You're from this town. Foley and I were just about to figure out who all I knew and how they correlate with those that Cavanagh knows."

Will snorted at that. Cavanagh knew just about everyone in their small town. That made it difficult to determine who might be after her. He frowned for a moment before he shook his head. This attack was personal, both of them, and it involved a close friend and now a new friend. He had no idea where to start looking for Cavanagh.

Chapter 13

A day later, Cleary stared down at the material that they had started to amass. There was not a lot. He had spent time researching the Lockyer house, dismayed at what he found. The house had been rumoured to have been a hideout for criminals over its long history. There had been no proof of that, however. Cleary stared across his office, lost in thought, before he set those papers aside and turned to his own work. He had contacted his clients and agreed to work as he could. Foley had simply told him that he had friends and other men who would step in to help in to help him. He had been grateful for that.

Sorting through what he needed to do, Cleary rose at last and stretched before he reached for his crutches. He frowned as he heard the front door bell. He was not expecting anyone. Thumping that way, Cleary stared out the door window before he reached to unlock it and open it.

"Will? Is this over yet? Is Cavanagh home?" Cleary was hopeful that she was.

"Not yet. I have a friend here who would like to speak with you." Will motioned to the youth standing beside him. "He's looking to get into your line of work and has the agreement of his high school to work with you if you'll let him. You would be reimbursed for this." Will grinned at the look on Cleary's face.

"What are you talking about?" Cleary stepped back to let them in.

"Jeff here is in his last year of high school and is planning on taking the surveyor's course to become certified, just as you are. He wants to gain some experience in it. As I said, his high school has agreed to let him earn credits if you are willing to employ him as a sort of apprentice over the next few weeks while you are healing. You do need help. If it matters, I can vouch for him." Will took Jeff's coat and hung it in the hall closet along with his own, setting their shoes to one side on a tray. "A bonus is that Jeff's father is the town historian and he can help you to understand the history of the town and in particular, the Lockyer house."

Cleary's head swivelled to stare at Jeff who grinned at him and then nodded.

"That's true. Dad has been pulling what he knows about the house. He asked me to have you call him if you were interested." Jeff handed over a business card. "Now, may I work with you?" His grin was infectious.

Cleary stared at him for a moment before he too grinned. Will watched them, satisfied that he had come up with a solution for both of them. He waved as he walked away, knowing that he was not needed in this discussion.

Cleary pointed towards the kitchen and thumped that way. Jeff followed, a troubled smile on his face for the moment. He wasn't sure what he could do for Cleary but he was willing to do his best to help out and also learn as well.

"Talk to me, Jeff." Cleary was reaching for bread and sandwich meat, an eye on the clock.

"What do you want to know?" Jeff reached to help, having been taught well by his parents.

"Whatever you can tell me. Tell me about yourself, your hopes and your dreams." Cleary bowed his head to pray for their food and Jeff just followed his lead.

Jeff began to speak as they ate, telling Cleary about his parents and his younger sister. He told him of his dreams to be like Cleary, a surveyor. He also spoke about his friends and how they had formed a group to help out those who needed their assistance around their homes.

Cleary listened intently to Jeff, reaching for a pad of paper to make notes. He nodded as he heard Jeff's words.

"Okay, then, Jeff. Who do I talk to at your school about your cooperative studies with me? And I will take you on after you graduate and while you are at school. I'm at the point where I can use some help." Cleary grinned as Jeff pumped his fist in the air. "We'll start on Monday. In the meanwhile, I would like to talk with your dad."

"I figured that you would. He's around this weekend and asked me to tell you that. He also asked if you could come for a meal? That way we can all work on this."

"That would be wonderful. Thank you, Jeff."

Late that evening, Cleary stretched out on his couch, an arm across his eyes. He was exhausted but his mind would not stop working. His thoughts tossed around the information that he had been provided by Jeff's father, Aaron. He would need to sort through the paperwork that he had been provided with. His hand relaxed as he slept. The paperwork slipped from his hand and fluttered to the floor.

Cleary didn't hear the chiming of his phone or the tapping at his front door. Will was looking for him and frustrated that he could not find him or rouse him if he was at home and asleep. He turned away from the door and headed for his own home. Will needed to rest as well and come back on Monday refreshed and ready to fight on.

There had been no sign of Cavanagh. There was also no work on her. They were actively looking for her. Friends were out and putting up missing posters. There was a tip line that had been set up and they were working through the tips that were coming in.

Foley lifted his mug up to sip at his coffee. He was more than worried about his daughter but all he could do was to pray for her safety and for her return to them. He knew that Dagen was around somewhere, just not with him.

Dagen stood and stare at the Lockyer house, a frown on his face. He had been drawn back there, searching for his granddaughter or at least some answers. That was not happening. He didn't hear the hushed footsteps that approached him. A slight sound behind him had him turning, an arm up to protect himself. Only that didn't work. A blow to his head sent him to the ground. The man looked around and then dragged Dagen's body over to the edge of the yard and into some brush. He searched for Dagen's keys and then ran for Dagen's truck, heading off with it. The truck that he had arrived in followed him.

The night grew dark and cold. Only God knew where Dagen was and how seriously he was hurt. Alarm would be raised the next morning when he didn't appear for his usual Saturday morning breakfast with Foley.

Chapter 14

The next morning, Foley pounded at his father's front door before he reached with a fumbling hand to unlock the door. He almost ran through the house, not finding his father. He paused in the backyard, looking around. Dagen's truck was in the driveway but he was not home. Foley didn't think that he had been around overnight. There just didn't seem to be any evidence of that.

Foley reached for his phone and scrolled through his messages. There was nothing from his father. He then reached to call in to the police detachment for help. Dagen had disappeared, just as Cavanagh had.

Will caught the call from his supervisor as he was wandering through the grocery store. He stared at his phone in shock before he was running from the store, his groceries forgotten. He ran from his parked car to where he saw Foley standing on the front porch.

"Foley? What is this?" Will slid to a halt in front of the older man.

"Dad's missing. He's not here but his truck is. I don't understand." Foley was deeply worried about his father's disappearance.

"Where would he have gone then?" Will studied the yard in front of him.

"I have no idea." Foley reached for his phone. "Dad?"

Dagen's voice was faint enough that Foley was having trouble hearing him.

"Foley? Can you come and get me? I'm at the Lockyer place." His phone clicked off, leaving Foley and Will staring at one another.

"Did he say the Lockyer place?" Will grabbed at Foley's arm, tugging him towards his car. "Get in, Foley. I'll get us there quicker." Will took off with the siren and lights activated. He pulled into the overgrown driveway, noting more tire tracks than before. Someone had been in and out just in the last couple of days.

Foley was out of the vehicle almost before Will had come to a stop, running for the front steps where his father had seated himself. He crouched before his father, a hand resting on his forearm.

"Dad?" Foley's voice brought Dagen's head up. He drew in a deep breath at the whiteness of his father's face.

"Foley? You're here?" Dagen's voice was slow and wavering. He staggered as he stood, not steady on his feet.

"I am, Dad. Why are you?" Foley's arm was around his father, guiding him to Will's car. The two younger men shared a look, worry on both of their faces.

Will headed for the hospital, waiting as Foley helped his father from the car and then headed back for the Lockyer house. He was well aware that other officers would be there and searching for any sign of any evidence.

Foley refused to leave his father's side and the physician allowed it. He watched as his father was assessed and an intravenous line was started. His father had been out overnight from his mutterings.

Will stared around the yard of the Lockyer place. What was it about this place that caused all of this heartache, he wondered? He looked up, begging for a sign from God. This would have to be solved that way, he decided. His prayers were constant for his friends.

Dagen roused late that afternoon, pulling up the covers to try and warm himself. His eyes rested on his son where he sat near his father's bed.

"Foley?" Dagen's voice roused Foley from his thought.

"Dad? What happened?"

"I'm not sure, son. I went out to the Lockyer house yesterday, just to look at it and see if I could make any sense of what was happening. I heard a small noise and don't remember anything until I woke up this morning and called you." He looked down at his clasped hands. "Where's my truck?"

"At your home." Foley frowned at his father. "Who did that? It's what happened with both Cavanagh and Cleary. Their vehicles were returned to their homes."

"They were, even though the work van should have gone to the shop." Foley frowned at his father. "I wonder why it wasn't returned to there."

"That's a good question, Foley." Will came to a stop beside the bed. "That's something that we're working on. Now, Dagen, what else can you say?"

Dagen shook his head. He had already said what he could to Will before Will had walked away to start his investigation into this. He didn't like that Dagen had been harmed.

Before Dagen had reached out to Foley, he had roused somewhat in the early morning hours before losing consciousness again. It was light when he roused once more and sat up, feeling the dampness of the night covering him. He finally rose to his feet, staggering to the front steps and collapsing on them. Dagen reached at last for his phone, calling his son. His head dropped as he waited for Foley to appear. He had no idea who had attacked him the day before and then left him to die in the brush. God had protected him, he knew. He just wished that he had the keys that were needed to unlock the mysteries that were surrounding them.

Will nodded. He had suspected that he would not get much information from Dagen. He had spent hours at the Lockyer house, searching with the officers. There were just no signs of anyone else being there other than tire tracks. And those were not clear enough for the techs to get any castings of the tires.

Dagen's head went back on the pillows. He slept, not hearing the quiet conversation between Foley and Will. Both of the men were puzzled by the events. There was something about that house that kept pulling Cavanagh, her family, and Cleary into its depth. There were only rumours about the background of the house and the people who had lived there.

Chapter 15

Day by day went by. Days turned into weeks until six weeks had gone by. The three men in Cavanagh's life searched earnestly for her, just not finding her. Will worked diligently as best he could to find her and to solve the mystery of why it had happened. He wasn't able to and that frustrated him to no end. He kept in daily contact with the three men who simply shrugged and walked away when he asked how they were.

Foley had simply moved in with his father, needing that closeness. Dagen was growing older each day and seemed to be more frail. The worry and stress of not having his granddaughter home was weighing heavily on him. Foley in turn watched for any sign of his daughter everywhere he went, whether on the job or on personal time.

Cleary was working as hard as he could, desperate to forget about Cavanagh. That didn't work out as well as he had prayed that it would. Jeff worked quietly along with him, wanting to learn as much as he could. Cleary was happy to have help as he worked. He had spent hours with Jeff's father, going over the history of the town and that of the Lockyer house. There just wasn't any proof as to the rumours of the criminal activities that had gone on there.

Walking towards his car one day, Cleary paused. He had been able to get rid of the cast but was still cautioned to take care. It would be a while before he could take up his daily runs once more. He looked up at the sky that was filled with rain clouds. Cleary sighed. It had been dreary and rainy for the last week and he was tired of it. He wanted blue skies and warmth. He was also deeply worried about Foley and Dagen. He could see the damage that was being done by Cavanagh's continued disappearance. He also wanted that lady home. She intrigued him and he wanted to pursue a relationship with her. That was not Cleary. He didn't date, not wanting to give an impression that he was interested in any particular lady.

Foley looked around that afternoon, his thoughts as usual on his daughter. He had spent the night before on his knees, petitioning God to return his daughter to him in good health and alive. He had had to come to terms that he might never see her again or that she might come home and they would be facing a funeral.

On his feet, Foley walked towards the front door of the shop, opening it to stare outside into the parking lot. He was certain that he had heard a vehicle and then Cavanagh's voice. Only, she wasn't there. Foley frowned before he headed back to reach for his jacket and then walked back outside. He stood for a moment and stared at the shop. Was it really worth it to keep it going? Was the shop the reason that his beloved daughter had disappeared? He shook his head before he stared down at the pavement that he was standing on. Something was wrong out there, Foley decided. He just didn't know what.

Foley paced around the building. He knew that Dagen was out and changing locks on a house. He had taken the work van. Foley's car and Dagen's car were still in the lot. He frowned at them before he stared back at the cars. Something seemed off there, he decided, and walked that way. He walked around his car and didn't see anything. A soft sound had him spinning to stare at Dagen's car. He realized then that there was someone in the car. Dagen was always forgetting to lock his vehicle. Suspecting a crime in progress, Foley wrenched open the door to stop and stare at the person there.

On his knees, Foley's hands reached for Cavanagh. He didn't know how she got there but there she was. His hand rested on her cheek, a prayer on his lips, and tears on his own face. Reaching for his phone, he called for help before he called Dagen.

"Dad? How close to being finished are you?" Foley's voice shook with his emotions.

"Just pulling into the lot, son. What's wrong?" Dagen pulled the van to a stop beside Foley's car before he was out of the van and bending over with an arm around Foley's shoulders. "Cavanagh? How? When?"

"Just now, I think, Dad. I heard a sound and came out. Thank goodness you forgot to lock your car. But I don't understand why she's in the car and not in the shop." Foley was on his feet and moving back to let the emergency personnel have space to work on Cavanagh.

Dagen's arm remained around his son before he was away and locking up the shop. He was back beside his son, watching as Cavanagh was transferred to a stretcher and then wheeled rapidly away. Dagen's hand pulled his son to his car and shoved him inside, reaching for his keys. He drove off, following the ambulance. The two men ran towards the hospital entrance, desperate to find out how Cavanagh was.

Will turned as he heard his name called. He had walked towards a nearby diner, needing a meal. A patrol officer was running towards him.

"Will? We've been trying to reach you. Cavanagh was found at the locksmith shop."

Will stared at him in shock, not taking in that Cavanagh had reappeared.

"What did you say?"

"Cavanagh. Her father found her in her grandfather's car just a bit ago. She's at the hospital."

Will turned and walked rapidly towards his car, listening to the information that the officer was giving him. He sped towards the hospital, praying that Cavanagh would be able to speak with him. His steps paused as he reached for his phone. He took it upon himself to contact Cleary.

"Cleary? Where are you?" Will's voice was rushed sounding.

Cleary stared at his phone and then at Jeff. They had just returned to his office and were tidying up from the day.

"At my shop. What's up?"

"It's Cavanagh. She's at the hospital. Foley found her just a bit ago in Dagen's car."

“How?” Cleary stared at Jeff in shock, who was staring back at him. “I’m on my way.”

Jeff was at his side as he ran for his truck, hopping in as Cleary took off. The two men ran for the hospital entrance, finding Will waiting for them.

“Will? Any word?” Cleary was hopeful.

“Not that I know of. They’re assessing her now, Foley tells me.” Will’s hand stopped Cleary. “Cleary? I don’t know what you’re feeling for Cavanagh. I suspect that you do have feelings for her. We’ll work with that. Now, go ahead and find Foley and Dagen.” Will shared a look with Jeff who gave a nod.

Chapter 16

Foley's feet bounced on the tiled floor of the waiting room. He wanted to be with his daughter but had been prevented from that. He could feel people around him but refused to take his eyes away from the door.

Cleary watched Foley carefully before he shared a look with Dagen. Dagen's face held hope but also sorrow. He had not wanted this to end this way. He had wanted Cavanagh to walk back into their lives, on her feet. Cleary's attention then went to Will who stood nearby, in conversation with an officer. He frowned for a moment, not fully comprehending what had happened. He wasn't convinced if any of them knew.

Foley was on his feet as a nurse approached, Dagen beside him, ready to find his daughter. Dagen's hand reached for Cleary's arm and pulled him with them, leaving Jeff staring at the three men before he pulled out his phone and called his father.

Foley approached his daughter's stretcher, a hand out to rest against her hair. It was hard to believe that she was here and with them. He had not expected it. His eyes raised for a moment as he begged God to forgive his lack of faith and belief before his eyes were on Dagen and then Cleary. He nodded. It was right that Cleary was there.

"Doc? What can you tell us?" Dagen's voice broke into the silence.

“Right now? Not a lot. I wanted you three to be with her. We’re still running tests and blood work. I don’t know why she won’t wake up. That’s part of what we’re investigating. Now, there are no broken bones or anything like that. The ligaments in the shoulder have healed nicely. We’ll be in and outer the next while. You can stay with her.” The physician walked away, puzzled at Cavanagh’s appearance. It had not been expected in that way.

Will stopped the physician for a few words before he nodded and headed for Cavanagh’s room. He understood only too well what they were looking for. That frightened him and not much frightened him after his years as an officer.

Foley walked away after an hour. He had to. His emotions were over the top and he had to take a break. He looked back at his father, seeing Dagen slumped into a chair. Cleary had already walked away, finding Jeff and Jeff’s father, Jake, waiting for him. They had headed for the cafeteria, Jake wanting to speak with Cleary

Will was waiting for Foley, a hand out to draw him away from the people milling around the waiting room. He drew him into a small conference room that he had taken over before he shoved Foley into a chair. He sat as well, his notebook out on the table. He prayed for his friends before he looked at Foley. Will drew in a deep breath at the devastation and worry that was on his friend’s face.

“Foley? What can you tell me?”

Foley shrugged, not sure what to say. He had just spoken with the physician, who had not been optimistic as to when Cavanagh would make up. Foley had nodded, feeling his father beside him as the physician spoke to them. Cavanagh would be moved to a room on the medical floor at some point. Both Foley and Dagen had been adamant that they would not be leaving her side. The physician had nodded, his eyes on Will who stood nearby. Will had already informed him that an officer would be at Cavanagh's door all the time. The physician had not been shocked at that. He had expected it, given what he knew.

"Will? What do you know?" Foley didn't think that he would find out anything but he had to ask any way.

"Not a lot, Foley. I need to speak with her before I can make any kind of sense as to what happened." Will had been back to the Lockyer house to walk around it and then to stand and stare at it, praying that he would find answers. Those answers were not found. He was aware that no ransom demand had not been received. That puzzled him as well.

"Where was she, Will? How did she just reappear as she did? She's lost weight. There is scraping on her ankle as well. What caused that?" Foley stared at the floor, not wanting to know the reasons for that scrape.

"The injury? It appears that she had had a shackle on that ankle that kept her from running away." Will winced at the look on Foley's face. "We can't be sure about that but we will confirm it when we speak with Cavanagh."

“I wish I knew who it was. They need to be brought to justice.” Foley knew that his anger had to be surrendered to God and that God alone had the keys to solving this. “Where’s Cleary?”

“He’s with Jeff and Jake. He’s really taken Jeff under his wing.” Will was happy that Cleary was doing that with Jeff.

“I’m glad. Jeff needs that.”

Will became lost in thought, not hearing Foley rise and walk away. He looked up at last as a thought crossed his mind. He was walking away from the hospital, not seeing Cleary waiting to speak with him.

Cleary sighed. He had wanted to speak with Will but that didn’t seem possible at the moment. He turned and headed for his car before he drove away and headed for his home. He would be back the next day, praying that Cavanagh would be awake then.

The next morning, Cavanagh shifted on the bed, gradually awakening. She grew still as she listened the faint sounds that hit her ears. She could smell the faint antiseptics that surrounded her. Cavanagh’s eyes opened and she squinted against the light. Her gaze moved around the room. A hospital room? When did that happen? Cavanagh began to weep silently. She was free. Only God could have opened the locked door that had held her captive for all those weeks.

Arms surrounded her as she wept and she heard a man praying for her. It wasn’t her father or grandfather, she knew. The hold was different. She listened and recognized Cleary’s voice. How could that be, she wondered? He was dead, wasn't he? That's what she had been told.

When she could control her emotions, Cavanagh leaned back to look up at Cleary. Her hands gripped his arms tightly. She frowned at the look on his face and in his eyes.

"Cleary?" Her voice was rough from the silence that she had been forced to keep over the past six weeks.

"Cavanagh? You're here. Are you okay?" Cleary studied the lady who he had admitted had become important to him.

"I don't know. What happened? How did I get here?" Cavanagh was puzzled and scared.

"We don't know. You appeared in your grandfather's car yesterday afternoon. You were unconscious. Don't say anything yet. Will needs to get your statement." Cleary tightened his hold on her as she began to shake.

"I don't know where I was. I was kept in a room. It was horrible, Cleary. They kept me shackled even though the door was locked. He wasn't going to let me go." Cavanagh's fear continued to grow. Nothing that Cleary said helped until he began to pray for her and to sing some of the old-time hymns that he loved so much.

Cavanagh's terror began to fade as she felt the peace that only God could give wafting through her soul and heart. She slept, leaving Cleary holding her. He looked around as Will entered.

"Cleary?" Will walked to the end of the bed. "Cavanagh's been awake?"

"She has been. She said that she had been shackled in a locked room and that he, whoever he is, wasn't going to let her go. Cavanagh didn't recognize the place but I'm not sure she was able to see much."

"That's likely what happened." Will was torn. He wanted to wait for Cavanagh to wake up again but he had other investigations to work on. "Call me when she awakens again. Don't let her talk."

"She won't. She already said that she couldn't." Cleary stared at Will. "How do we find out where she was? Is that even possible?"

"We're trying, Cleary. We are trying. Where are Dagen and Foley?"

"They had to work. They didn't want to but they had to." Cleary's eyes were back on Cavanagh and didn't see the look that Will shot his way before he walked away.

Chapter 17

Will watched Cavanagh closely later that day. She was avoiding eye contact with him, her eyes on her hands instead. He had asked her father to leave so that he could speak with her. Will knew that Foley was just outside the door, waiting impatiently for her interview to finish. It just didn't seem as if it would even begin.

"Cavanagh. You need to talk to me. And now." Will was stern with her, knowing that he had to be.

"I know, Will. I know. I just don't know where to start. I can't remember what happened to me when I disappeared."

Will told her, watching her with compassion as her face crumpled for a moment.

"It is what it is, Cavanagh. Yes, Cleary was hurt once more. He would rather have been the one who disappeared, not you. That didn't happen. We now have to get your statement and then go from there. So, what happened to you? It's been six weeks since you disappeared."

Cavanagh blinked back her tears. She had to talk. Only she didn't want to. She didn't want to admit how afraid that she was. Her father and grandfather had been threatened as had Cleary. Cavanagh raised her head to look at Will, finding him watching her in return. She began to pray harder than she had ever prayed before.

"I can't remember how I disappeared, Will. And I don't remember what happened for at least three days." Cavanagh looked up at him, a shuttered look on her face but fear in her eyes. "Where do I start?"

"Just start with what you first remember. We can work on filling in the gaps as we go along. Let me pray with you first." Will did just that, his head not raising when he finished. He was troubled by what Cavanagh had gone through. He knew that this had changed her. Will was working through who he could connect her with for counselling.

Cavanagh stared at her hands once more, her thoughts tumbling over and over. Her mouth opened and closed multiple times before she could scrape up the courage to start to speak.

"I don't know where to start, Will. I don't remember being taken or for the first few days. I think it might have been the third day I was there."

On that day, Cavanagh had roused, rolling to her side and rubbing at her face. She shoved her tangled hair away from her face before she sat up. She peered around the room before she stumbled towards the bathroom. She didn't feel the shackle on her ankle or hear the sound of it as it dragged across the floor.

Cavanagh slumped back on the bed, her eyes closing before she even realized where she was or that she was a prisoner. She reached for the blanket to pull it up over her and then slept. She didn't hear the rattling of a key in the lock or the squeaking of the hinges at the door opened. Cavanagh was not aware that she was in a room in the attic from which she could not escape. It would take days for her to realize that. The drug that had sedated her had been kept up over the last few days. Part of that was to try and break her spirit.

The woman who appeared shuffled across the floor to stand and stare down at the younger woman. Her hard living and love of alcohol, tobacco, and drugs showed on her face. Nicotine stained the fingers that she raised to touch Cavanagh's face. Cavanagh flinched away from her touch and moved away from her in her sleep. The woman sneered at her before she looked around the room. She picked up the tray that sat by the bed and walked away. She would be back in a short while with another tray that Cavanagh would not touch.

A day later, Cavanagh sat on the side of the bed. She was somewhat more alert. A hand rubbed at her shoulder, finding it painful. She frowned as she stared around the room. She didn't recognize it at all. Cavanagh was on her feet, heading for the door. She frowned once more as she came to a halt. She stared down at her ankle before she sat on the floor and reached for her ankle.

Cavanagh tugged at the shackle, not able to dislodge it or remove it. She began to panic. She had no idea why this had happened or why it had been done. She was on her feet, searching for anything that she could use to jimmy the lock and release herself. There was not one thing that she could use. Whoever had planned this room for her had taken steps to ensure that she could not escape.

Her thoughts were troubled. She had no idea what day it was or how long that she had been imprisoned in that room. On her feet, she paced to the window and stared down. An attic, she thought. There is no way that a way of escape would happen. Cavanagh turned to study the room once more, finding only the bare amount of furniture in it. She was frustrated and afraid. As she had been taught, her thoughts turned to prayer and she felt the peace of God filtering into her heart.

Pacing the room, Cavanagh tried hard to come up with a way to escape. She just couldn't. She finally slumped back on the bed and slept, not hearing the door open once more and the woman appear.

The woman, Jane by name, had been under orders to have Cavanagh on her feet and ready to meet the woman's employer. That wasn't going to happen, she could tell. She cursed loudly before she stomped away, the door slammed and locked behind her before she thumped down the stairs. She crept towards the office where she knew that her employer was and hesitated at the door. No one entered the office without being told to enter.

The man worked away, knowing full well that Jane was there. He was deep in nefarious deeds and didn't need her distracting him.

"What is it, Jane?" His voice was harsh as he spoke, not raising his eyes at all.

"She's still sleeping. I can't wake her up." Jane's voice had become a whine, a whine that grated on the man's nerves and made him wish that he had hired someone else. Unfortunately, Jane was a relative and he had promised her mother that he would employ her. He regretted that promise.

"And why not?"

"She was given too much of the sedative. It should have been stopped earlier."

"That was not your decision. Have her on her feet tomorrow to meet with me. It will not go well with you if she's not." He just continued with his work. He didn't think that it would be any loss if he had to get rid of her. And if she didn't comply with his wishes, that is exactly what would happen to her.

Jane nodded before she walked away. She was angry, more angry than she had ever been. She knew how her employer thought. Others had disappeared because they failed to comply with his wishes. She didn't want to be one of them.

Chapter 18

Staring at Jane, Cavanagh simply kept her seat on the bed. She didn't move from where she had planted herself that morning. She felt grungy, she decided, but there was no way for her to shower or bath. The shackle kept her from doing that.

Jane stared at Cavanagh, unsettled by the calmness that Cavanagh showed. She should not be like that. Any other female who had been shackled in that room had been frantic and afraid, trying hard to escape. Cavanagh was not doing that.

"What do you want?" Cavanagh's voice was firm.

"You. You are to come with me." Jane's hand reached for the shackle and unlocked it. Her hand kept a tight grip on Cavanagh's good arm, shoving her towards the door and then down the steps.

Cavanagh had difficulty keeping her balance. She couldn't use either hand due to the sling on one arm and the grip on the other. Jane sneered behind Cavanagh's back, knowing that the younger lady was in her control. Shoved forward once she reached the first floor, Cavanagh came to a stop at the office doorway and was forced to stand there. Her mind was working, taking in as much as she could. She locked away a description of Jane in her mind before she turned to the man in the office. Her breath almost stopped for a moment. She knew the man. He was evil, she knew. She had been kept away from wherever he would be. Now? Now, she was in his presence. Cavanagh felt the evil in the house and in that office.

The man lifted his head, his gold pen dropping to the desk top. He was on his feet, facing Cavanagh. He frowned, seeing the defiance that she was showing as well as the calmness that she felt. That would change and soon, he decided. He would drive that from her and in just a day or so. That wouldn't take much effort.

"Welcome to my home, Cavanagh. I've been waiting for you to visit." His voice was oily and evil.

Cavanagh snorted at his words, bringing anger to his face.

"I highly doubt that, Webster. You didn't bring me here for my health or my good. You're evil and everyone knows that." Cavanagh rocked on her feet at the blow that was launched across her face. "Go ahead. Beat me up. Kill me. I won't ever do what you want." Cavanagh was shaking inside but calm on the outside.

Ivan Webster stared at her. Her defiance had been unexpected. He had been convinced that keeping her sedated would weaken her and then frighten her. That didn't seem to have worked. He looked past her at Jane and then waved her away. He turned back to his desk, seeking to come up with a new plan of attack. He would break her spirit and do that soon.

Cavanagh was yanked roughly from the room. She twisted her arm and freed it. She shoved at the woman and caused her to tumble to the floor. Cavanagh fled for the front door, wrenching open the locks and then running through the doorway and down the steps. It didn't matter that she was in her bare feet.

She sprinted across the front lawn, heading for the road and prayed that someone would stop and help her.

Not hearing the running footsteps behind her, Cavanagh screamed as arms were wrapped around her and stopped her forward run to safety. She screamed and then fought the man holding her as best that she could with only one arm. Her fingernails scratched at him and her feet kicked at him. She could hear the curses from him and then the threats.

Cavanagh continued to struggle to escape even as she was forced back up the stairs and to the room in the attic. She was dropped abruptly to the floor and held there as the shackle was fastened once more around her ankle. Her head dropped as the door was slammed behind them and the lock snapped into place.

She slumped on the floor, her breathing rough from her struggles. Her eyes closed as she prayed. She had tried hard to get away but had not succeeded. That would not mean that she would give up and just accept her fate. She would find the key to unlock her door of captivity and take that chance to escape.

Rising after what seemed like hours, Cavanagh was on her feet, heading for the bathroom to find a hot cloth to wipe at her face. She slumped back on the brd, her emotions running wild. Her eyes closed as she begged God to release her and let her go back to her family. She slept, not hearing the door unlock and the woman entering.

The woman stood by the bed and stared down at Cavanagh. To have her try and escape like that had been unexpected. They had all expected that she would just go along with them. Any other female would not have tried that, especially if they were injured. The man had been angry at Jane. He blamed her for Cavanagh's escape attempt.

Webster had been angry at the disturbance that Cavanagh had caused. He blamed both Jane and the man for that. He stomped away from the house and drove away, shouting that they had better not let it happen again.

Jane walked away from the room, determined that Cavanagh would cave to the demands that would be made and that she would do that quickly. She underestimated Cavanagh. Cavanagh would not submit to any of those demands.

Cavanagh roused a few hours later. She snuggled under the blankets, her eyes closing once more. Her shoulder was paining her but she didn't have any medications to take for it. Not that she would even if she was offered them.

Webster returned late that night. Things had not gone well for him that day in his meetings. He was frustrated and that frustration was taken out on those around him.

Jane followed him just as a puppy dog would, looking for confirmation that she was not to blame for what had happened. She didn't speak. Her words would not have been answered and Webster would have just told her to shut up. She finally sought her own rest, anger towards Cavanagh growing. Jane was determined that Cavanagh would pay for that day. It may take her a while but she would exact her revenge on her.

Webster stared at the paperwork in front of him. Things were not going well for him at the moment. Pressure was building all around him and he wanted to leave the small town. He was already planning his escape. Cavanagh had become part of that. She just didn't know it as yet.

Chapter 19

Day followed dreary day. Cavanagh was released from her shackle every day and dragged down the stairs to stand in Webster's office. Jane and one of the men who were always around took great care that Cavanagh did not have any chance to escape again. The man stood at the entry to the office. Jane stood tight to Cavanagh, a hand gripping her arm as hard and as tight as she could.

Webster didn't look at Cavanagh directly. He studied her, however, trying to determine just how to approach her. She was difficult to reach, he decided, and not like his usual captives. They alway caved to his demands and commands within a few days. Cavanagh was not cooperating with him. He frowned as he saw the peace and confidence that she showed. That shouldn't be happened.

Five weeks into her captivity, Jane approached her with a dress, jewelry and makeup in her arms. She had been told that Cavanagh was to be dressed in the new clothing with her hair and make up done.

Cavanagh looked at the dress and the accessories and simply refused to touch them. She had a good idea what Webster was up to. She was not going to go along with him.

Jane fought her to try and get her dressed. Cavanagh fought back, determined that she would not play the games that Webster wanted her to play. A sudden shove from Jane sent Cavanagh off balance. She fell, her head hitting against the door frame to the bathroom. She slumped to the floor, her eyes closing as she lost consciousness.

Jane stared at her in horror. She shook her and then ran for a cold washcloth to slap against her face. Nothing worked to rouse Cavanagh. Jane was on her feet, backing towards the door, and then through it. She slammed and locked the door. Her steps were quiet and slow as she descended the stairs, not wanting to face Webster.

Webster finally looked around at Jane, frowning at her.

"What's the problem, Jane?" His voice was loud and harsh.

"Cavanagh struggled with me and fell. She's unconscious. She won't be able to be at your meal tonight." Jane shrank back from the violent anger that covered Webster's face. "She just wouldn't dress as you wanted her to. She fought me."

Webster didn't speak. In fact, he couldn't speak. His rage grew until he threw the glass of liquor directly at Jane, who ducked and then backed out of the room. Her experience had taught her that she needed to disappear for a few days to let Webster cool off. Jane just wasn't sure that he would cool off enough for her to be around him.

Webster's curses filled the downstairs of the house. No one came around him. In fact, everyone had fled the house, leaving him on his own. Webster himself left the house soon after that. He was due to leave for a trip that would take him out of the country for two weeks. He really didn't care at that if

Cavanagh was taken care of or not. He would find out when he returned in two weeks. Perhaps by that time, she would be more than willing to cooperate with him.

The next week went by with no one in the house. Cavanagh waited each day for a tray of food to appear. It didn't. She paced her room, wondering why Jane had not appeared to drag her down the stairs to stand for ages in Webster's office. She began to grow weak from lack of food. By the time that the seven or eight days had passed, Cavanagh was not moving around, staying on the bed and sleeping.

Cavanagh didn't hear the cautious steps that approached the door and unlocked it. The man shoved it open and then stood just inside the open doorway to study Cavanagh. He was across the room after a moment, a hand out to feel Cavanagh's wrist, grateful that she was alive. He reached for the shackle and worked a key in the lock. It dropped away from Cavanagh's ankle. The man held her ankle to study the scrapings on it before he scooped Cavanagh into his arms and turned to leave the room. He closed and locked the door behind them before he quickly walked down the stairs and across the front lawn to his truck. Cavanagh was tucked inside the car before the man was running away to climb inside his truck and drive away.

Heading for the locksmith shop, the man hesitated. He didn't want to be the one who dropped Cavanagh back into the family. He didn't want his name out there. He was out of the truck and around to the passenger side. The man looked around and then headed for Dagen's car. It was unlocked, for which he was thankful. He dropped Cavanagh to the front seat and then shut the door. He looked around, pulling the cap down further over his face before he was running for his truck and driving away. He was confident that Cavanagh would be found and found soon. He looked around to find a spot where he could monitor the lot and watch the activity there.

Watching the activity that grew in the lot as Cavanagh was found and then transported away, the man breathed a sigh of relief. His fingers tapped on the steering wheel as he watched Will speaking with an officer before he nodded. He drove away, intending of finding Will at some point. It just wouldn't be that day.

Webster returned late that week, his business trip overseas successful, or so he thought. He walked heavily into his home and to his office, dropping his bags there. His head tilted as he listened and then frowned. He could hear no activity in the house and there should be. The lights had come on by the timers that had been set.

Walking through the house, Webster grew increasingly angry, There was no one there other than his personal valet and that man could tell him nothing about where the others were. Nor could the cook who appeared once more after he had returned to the house. Walking up the steps, his feet heavy on each stair, Webster unlocked the door to the attic room and entered. He stopped short, shock on his face as he saw the shackle but not Cavanagh. He searched for her before he was thundering down the stairs, calling for his cook. She appeared and then just shrugged at his shouted questions. She had no idea where Cavanagh was. Wasn't she locked up in the attic?

Webster stormed around his house. His curses were loud in the empty rooms. He had been married at one time but his wife had fled the home and disappeared. He had tried to track her but to no avail. He finally just stood and stared out of the window in his office. The light reflected around him, showing a man who was evil. His silhouette was as black as his heart.

Chapter 20

Cavanagh's thoughts returned to the present. She wiped at her face, not realizing that she had been weeping as she told her story. This was not her. She didn't cry, Will knew. It told how much of a toll that this captivity had taken on her and Will regretted it.

"Anything else?" Will waited patiently for Cavanagh to respond. He took notes of the names and descriptions of whoever it had been that was there. He was puzzled. Someone had released Cavanagh. He just didn't know who. Will suspected an employee of her captor but that would be hard to prove.

"Nothing, Will. I need to sleep." Cavanagh pulled the covers higher on herself and then slept, exhausted by the emotional and physical trauma that she had suffered.

Will tucked away his note pad and rose. He would get nothing else for Cavanagh, he knew. All he could do was pray for a touch of the garment on her and for the keys that were needed to unlock her story and find those responsible. Cavanagh had not known the name of the man who had kidnapped her. Her description had sounded very familiar to Will, but he could not put a name to the man.

Standing outside of the room, Cleary waited patiently for Will to appear. He needed to see his lady. Dagen and Foley had disappeared for now but would be back, he knew. His eyes were on Will's troubled face.

"Will?"

"She's sleeping, Cleary. Go on in. She needs to see you. In fact, you need to see her too." Will walked away without another word, leaving Cleary staring after him and then at Cavanagh's room. Cleary wanted to run after Will and force him to tell him what Cavanagh said. Only, he couldn't do that. That was part of the investigation. His eyes raised to study the ceiling, his prayers lifting for his lady. He then shoved open the door and walked in, finding a chair to sit and study Cavanagh, seeing the devastation and changes on her face.

Cleary slumped in his chair, not willing to leave Cavanagh on her own. He was convinced that she would disappear if he did so. His head turned slightly as he heard the door open before Foley and Dagen approached.

"Cleary?" Foley's voice had questions, the answers to which no one had.

"Will got her statement. He didn't say anything. Not that he could. She slept, I think, just as he was leaving." Cleary was on his feet. He had to leave, he knew, not being family. And that hurt. He wanted to be her family. That was new for him. He had had no interest in a lady, not until Cavanagh.

Cavanagh roused late that night, staring around the room. She was puzzled that she could move and not hear the noise or feel the pull of the shackle. She frowned as she took in the hospital room and then felt relief. Somehow, she had been freed. Cavanagh had no recollection of that. She wanted to find that person and thank them. Instead of being able to do that, she turned her thoughts to prayer. She clung to the promise that God frees the captive and heals them as well.

Foley was on his feet, a hand on his daughter's head. He was struggling with his emotions as he knew Dagen was as well. He studied Cavanagh and didn't like the changes that he saw in her. She was changed because of the past six weeks. They could not take back the lost time nor could they change Cavanagh back to who she was before that day.

Cavanagh jumped as she felt a hand on her face. She stared up at her father, her heart pounding before she drew a deep breath. Her family was safe, she could see. Dagen was asleep in a chair across the room.

"Cavanagh? Are you okay?" Foley kept his voice low, not wanting to disturb the silence in the room.

"No. No, I'm not, Dad. I want to know why and who is behind it all. I don't know that my kidnapper is the head of it all." Cavanagh swiped at the tears on her face.

"Will is working on that, love. We'll talk. For now, we need to let you rest and get rehydrated." Foley was saddened even more. "Grand will want to be on that conversation." He gave a small grin. "And I know that Cleary wants to be around you and find out what happened."

"He will. I just don't want anyone else hurt. I just don't know that we can avoid that." Cavanagh turned her attention to the intravenous bag hanging near her bed, the fluid dripping down the line to her hand. "How long was I gone, Dad?"

"Just over six weeks. We can't understand how you were just left in Grand's car instead of being brought into the shop."

"Someone didn't want you to know, I guess." Cavanagh was growing tired. "I'm sorry, Dad. I didn't have any food over the last week. I was left entirely on my own. I didn't see anyone." Cavanagh slept, not seeing the angry look on her father's face.

Dagen had roused at the two were talking. He too was puzzled by the events. He searched his mind to think of who that he could call in. He nodded. He had a friend who was an investigator. He had not reached out to him yet but the time had come to do that. Samuel would agree to work with him and would bring in his son, Blackie, and Blackie's friend, Simon. They would search through what they were told and find answers for them.

"Son?" Dagen's voice caused Foley to jump. "Is Cavanagh okay?"

Foley was shaking his head. She wasn't okay. And he didn't know how to fix it.

"She's not, Dad. She's changed. We'll never have our girl back."

"No, we won't." Dagen was saddened at that. "We'll not have her back but we have her with us. We'll adjust to the new Cavanagh. Cleary will be part of that if I am reading him correctly."

"I think that you are, Dad. They have made a connection that I don't see very often." Foley turned to face his father. "How do we help her?"

"I don't know, son. We'll work it through. We'll find someone for her to speak with. And Cleary will need that as well." Dagen was on his feet, reaching to hug his son. He could not take away the anger, hurt and sadness from him. Only God could do that.

"We will, Dad. You and I need to find someone to speak with as well. So, now what"

"Now what? We pray this through. We do what we can to help them both. We go on with our lives as best we can." Dagen turned as he heard a noise. "Cleary? Should you be here?"

"I have to be, Dagen. I need to be with her. Does that make any sense?" Cleary walked into the room and stood watching the two men.

"It does, Cleary. You care deeply for Cavanagh. You have made that crystal clear." Foley hugged the younger man. "I don't know where this is going with you two. If you both decide that you can't live without the other, we welcome you into the family."

The three men found chairs and circled them around the bed, leaving enough room for the medical staff to move around her bed.

Chapter 21

Two days later, Cavanagh glared at her father as they stood facing off against one another in the work shop. She was shaking her head. Foley didn't want her out working on her own. Cavanagh was determined to take back her life and to do that deed that very day.

"I have to, Dad. I can't let them win. If I hide away here or at home, they win. What else am I to do?" Her voice had a pleading tone to it that Foley had never heard before.

Dagen stood and watched the pair, knowing that Foley had valid fears but then Cavanagh had a valid reason to want to work. He shook his head even as he prayed for the two.

"Foley? Cavanagh? We need to think this through. Yes, Cavanagh needs to go back to her routine. She's right when she says that she can't hide. And we need her to pick her work back up again. We're that busy some days. All we can do is pray for her. And no, Foley, you can't go with her." Dagen grinned at his son for a moment. "God is in control. He has allowed what has happened. We don't know what the purpose is but He does. So, we sit and make plans. Cavanagh, grab our mugs of coffee and those doughnuts that you brought in. We'll go through the work orders and see what we do."

Foley nodded. His father was correct. He was trying to protect his daughter and in doing so was starting to smother her. That had never been allowed by either one of them.

"Dad's right, Cavanagh. Let's have that business meeting that we need to." He looked around as he heard the front door and peered into the reception area. He was not surprised to see Blackie there. He knew that Dagen had reached out to Samuel. "Blackie? Come on back. We're just about to have a business meeting that you need to be part of. How is Julia and the rest of your family?"

"We're all good." Levi Blackier, affectionally known as Blackie, reached to shake the men's hands and then gave Cavanagh a hug. He could understand to a certain extent what she was going through. He and three of his friends in Mistletoe had gone through what were termed as adventures but were more life and death than just an ordinary event. "I am glad to help where I can. We've been doing some research. I won the coin toss to come and update you on what we have."

"Blackie? You have news for us? I hope this solves it today. I want to go on with my life." Cavanagh glared at him for a moment as he just grinned at her. They were old friends, these two, even though life had caused them to drift in different directions.

"I do have information that we need to go over. I have copies for your investigator as well." Blackie dropped the files that he was holding onto the work table and took with thanks the coffee that was handed to him.

Dagen looked around at the other three and then simply bowed his head. He was well aware that prayer was the most formidable weapon that they had in their arsenal at the moment. God was in control and desired only the best for Cavanagh and Cleary. Sometimes, though, His best meant danger and harm and sometimes even death. They could not control that. They could only trust Him and move forward through each day, confident in Him.

Blackie raised his head to study Cavanagh when they had finished. He could see the loss of innocence on her face and in her eyes. That hurt, he knew. She would never be the same person that she had been. He searched his mind to think of who she could speak with and nodded. He knew just the lady and would reach out to her.

"Okay, Blackie, so what do we have?" Cavanagh simply stared at him, knowing that she likely didn't want to hear what he had to say. Her father's hand reached to give hers a quick clasp.

"Cavanagh? How be you tell me how you feel?" Blackie had been a medic in the armed forces and always felt that finding out how someone felt was the best step first.

"How do I feel?" Cavanagh blinked at him, not sure how to respond. "I'm hurt in so many ways. I'm angry. Confused. Desperate for answers. Wanting this over. Wanting to run away and hide until Will finds out whoever it is. Every emotion that you can think of? I've experienced. I'm terrified that they will go after Dad or Grand and hurt or kill them. I worry about Cleary. I know that he's just a new friend but we've become involved in something that has changed our lives both together and as individuals. Does that sound about right?"

"It does. It's what Julia and I experienced, Cavanagh. As did Jacob, Josh, and Simon. You know our stories. I have a lady in mind to contact who would be good for you to speak with. She and her husband had an adventure as well. She's a retired forensics psychologist but still is willing to speak with friends. She will consider you a friend."

"She will?" Cavanagh blinked at him before she nodded. "I would like that, I think. I need to know that I am not the only one who has undergone something. Perhaps she can help me find the keys to unlock the doors back to who I should be."

"Darcy can help with that, Cavanagh. She is one of the strongest Christian ladies that I know. She had a really rotten deal handed to her years ago but she came through victorious. Her husband is a police officer, which may help if you speak with him as well."

Cavanagh shrugged, not sure if that was an option or not. She found her father frowning at her and then her gaze caught the worried look that her grandfather was trying to hide.

"Blackie, what can you tell us?" Dagen kept his eyes on Cavanagh, not willing to look away.

"What can I tell you?" Blackie handed them each a folder. "Read through this and then we'll talk. It goes beyond Webster. That I think is what you expect."

Cavanagh read through the paperwork carefully. She could hear quiet comments between the three men. She flipped back to the first page and began to read once more. She was puzzled by what she was reading.

Hearing the front door open, she rose and headed that way, frowning at Cleary as he appeared.

"Cleary? What are you doing here? You're supposed to be working." Cavanagh surprised both of them by walking into the hug that he wasn't aware that he was offering.

"I had to come, Cavanagh. I can't do the job that I was to do today. Jeff's off with his friends. So I decided to come and find this friend of mine." He looked past her at Blackie, who had risen to ensure that Cavanagh was not in harm's way.

"Blackie, this is Cleary. You need to talk to him as well. Cleary, this is a friend of ours, Levi Blackier. We call him Blackie. He works for his father, who is a private investigator." Cavanagh reached for Cleary's hand and tugged him with her. "We were just going over what he brought. You need to see it as well." Cavanagh was back in her seat, Cleary dropping into a chair beside him.

Blackie handed over a folder to Cleary, assessing the man in front of him. He nodded. He would be able to tell his father that Cavanagh was safe with Cleary. That had been a concern of them all.

Dagen and Foley exchanged glances before Foley just shrugged. Cleary needed to be part of this discussion. They just had not expected him to be there at that point.

Chapter 22

Cavanagh paced her home that night. She was troubled by what Blackie had provided for them. He had been honest with them. Yes, he indicated, Webster was part of the group that was after Cavanagh. They just didn't have a clear picture of why. That didn't surprise any of them.

Cleary had watched Cavanagh closely as they listened to what Blackie had to say. Will had appeared as well at some point over the afternoon. He had taken Blackie to one side and spoke quietly with him, taking the information that he had given him. He assessed Cavanagh and Cleary. Will was worried about them, knowing that there were still people out there after them.

Cavanagh sighed out loud. She needed this over, she decided. She just didn't know how to do that. Cleary had walked away before they had finished their meeting with Blackie, needing to be at a meeting. She wanted to talk with him, to find out what his thoughts were. Tomorrow was Saturday. She was determined that she would track him down at some point and ask him just that.

Cleary yawned. He was exhausted physically but the emotional stress was heavier on him. He wanted to talk with Cavanagh but it was too late. His meeting had gone for hours. He would find her the next day.

Will was puzzled at the information that Blackie had provided. He wasn't sure how he and his father and friend had found this information. He would need to speak with him. He set aside the folder, intending on picking it up on Monday. He had been ordered not to work on the weekend and Will appreciated the fact that he needed a break.

Early the next morning, Cavanagh was sorting through the paperwork once more. Something puzzled her about the conclusions that she thought it was Simon had drafted. She read through his notes and then back through them. She frowned and then frantically began to make notes. Simon had included his email and she sent her notes off to him before she glanced at the clock. She groaned. It was not even six in the morning. That was really not cool, she decided, to send that email but she could not do anything about it now.

Simon grinned to himself as he read Cavanagh's questions. Blackie had warned Samuel and himself that she would be asking multiple questions as she struggled to understand the whys of what had happened and how to solve it. He responded to her questions as best he could. He decided that it might well mean a trip to her town over the next couple of days. He knew that his wife would be up for the trip and any others would be as well.

Cavanagh was surprised at the quick response from Simon. She had not expected that at all. She read through his email before she was printing off copies for the others involved in their adventure. She sat back when she was done, her thoughts troubled. Who was doing this? That she could not determine.

Cleary was on Cavanagh's doorstep, ringing the door bell. He knew that it was early but he could see lights on around the curtains. He waited almost impatiently for the lock to open. When it did, Cleary swept Cavanagh into a tight hug. He didn't want to let her go.

Cavanagh backed away at last, watching Cleary as he stepped inside and shut the door, locking it behind him. Cleary jacket and shoes were off before he walked towards Cavanagh, his head tilted to watch her.

"Cavanagh? What have you done?" Cleary winced as he spoke. He didn't mean to accuse her of anything but that was how it sounded.

"Just did some research. I read through the material over and over and then stopped on Simon's content. I sent him information and he has responded already. I printed everything off." She squinted at the clock. "It's early, Cleary."

"I know that it is." He lifted the bag that he was holding. "I stopped and picked up some breakfast for us."

"Thank you." Cavanagh headed for the kitchen and then turned. "What did you get?"

"Just pancakes and bacon. Does that work?"

"It is. Let's eat and then can we spend some time in prayer?" Cavanagh needed a prayer partner and right now, that appeared to be Cleary. She was hesitant to reach out to any of her friends just in case that put them at risk.

“We can do that.” Cleary helped to set out their meal before he reached to pour their juice. He sat, a hand reaching for Cavanagh’s hand. His head bowed as he hesitated for a moment. A vision of the two of them doing this for the rest of their lives shook him. He bit at his lip before he prayed. His head remained bowed for a moment before he looked up at Cavanagh, a smile just for her on his face.

An hour later, Cavanagh raised her head. She had felt the power and presence of God in the room and that hushed her fear. Cleary’s hand still held hers and she was reluctant to remove it.

“Cavanagh? Where’s the material?” Cleary was on his feet and headed for the office, returning with the piles of paper. “This is all of it?” He was amazed at the stack of paper.

“That is all of it. There is just so much.” Cavanagh felt confused and worried at the same time. “I don’t know what I’ve found, Cleary. I just pray that there is a key in there that unlocks this mystery.”

“We’ll find it, Cavanagh. I just pray that neither one of us is harmed again.” Cleary knew that was unlikely to happen. He prayed that they would be protected in whatever they faced.

“That’s what I am afraid of, Cleary. I’m praying that this is over with and soon. You need to get on with your life.” Cavanagh was on her feet and tidying away the garbage. She missed the look on Cleary’s face. She would have been very puzzled at it. It said that she was loved and cherished by him. Only he did realize that was what he was saying.

"We'll get through this, Cavanagh. With God's help, we'll get through it. We may not like what we have to face but we are not alone. Never alone." Cleary watched her closely, seeing how she relaxed for a moment at his words.

Chapter 23

Foley approached his daughter on the Monday morning, frowning at the strain that was showing on it. There were dark circles under her eyes that worried him. She moved away from him, not wanting to speak with him. Foley sighed before he reached for the work orders that were outstanding for that week. He flipped through them, knowing that Cavanagh would be out there on her own, doing what she was trained to do. And there was nothing that they could do that would stop them.

Cavanagh knew that her father wanted to talk with her. She wanted to talk with him as well. She just didn't know how to. She had handed both he and her grandfather the pile of material that she had amassed over the weekend the day before and then just walked away.

Turning as he heard the door open and then close, Foley peered into the reception area late that afternoon. He was surprised to see Simon Gardiner and his wife, Eavan, there.

"Simon? Welcome but what are you two doing here?"

"Good afternoon, Foley. Your daughter does. She sent me information on Saturday morning. We need to talk with her about that. Is she around?" Simon waved at Dagen who had appeared behind Foley.

“No, she’s not. She’s finishing up on a job site and then heading here.” Foley frowned. “In fact, she should be here now.” He walked away and out of the back door, breathing a sigh of relief as he saw Cavanagh tidying up the work van. “Cavanagh? Everything okay?”

“It is, Dad. It’s been a good day.” Cavanagh looked happy for the first time in weeks, he decided.

“That’s wonderful.” Foley reached to hug his daughter, holding on just a little bit longer and tighter. Changes were in the air for her and he could not be happy for her. “Simon and Eavan are here.”

Cavanagh blinked, surprised but was glad to hear that he was. She wanted to speak with him and had been about to jump in her car and head for Mistletoe.

“They are? I’m glad. We need to talk with him.”

“We do. Are you about finished out here?” Foley reached to close and lock the van door.

“I am, Dad. I need to clean up and then I’m ready to head for home. Or are we going to your place or Grand’s?”

“How be we head for your place? You have the information there on your computer, I suspect, and Simon will want to access that, I am sure.” Foley’s arm was around his daughter. “And we need to bring in Cleary. Do you know where he is?” He grinned at the frown that Cavanagh sent his way.

“I have no idea, Dad. Do you?” Cavanagh smirked at her father before she headed for the back door to the building and disappeared.

Foley's feet had come to a halt, a grin on his face. Cavanagh had not been joking with him like that for a while. He paused as he heard a vehicle and then shook his head. Cleary had appeared, just as he had expected him to. "Afternoon, Cleary."

"Foley? What are you doing? Waiting for me?" Cleary grinned at him.

"I guess I was. I'm certain that you are here to see Dagen." Foley just managed to hide his grin as Cleary's head shot around in disbelief.

Cleary's eyes narrowed before he grinned at Foley.

"Yes, that would be about right. I am here to see Dagen. Is he still here?" Cleary's laugh echoed behind him as he walked towards the door and disappeared.

Foley's own laugh broke out as he shook his head and then followed Cleary. A sound from behind him had him spinning but he could see no one. He frowned before he turned back to the building and disappeared into it as well.

Cavanagh jumped as she felt arms come around her and then felt a kiss on her cheek. Cleary had found her as she stood in the kitchen area of the building. She had been hesitant to find her grandfather. She could hear him speaking with Simon and Eavan.

"Cavanagh? Are you okay or are you hiding?" Laughter underlaid his voice.

Cavanagh shrugged. She was not sure what she was doing. She turned her head slightly to find Cleary's face near hers.

"I'm not sure what I'm doing any more, Cleary. I need to go out there. Only, I'm afraid to. I think that Dad wants to head to my home. I'm fine with that. I just don't like all this."

"None of us do, sweetheart. None of us do. Let's go find your friends and then head for your home. We'll work through what we can. And we will spend time in prayer. God is with us, sweetheart, and He holds the keys to unlocking all of this. It is in His time, though. As much as we want this over, we can't run ahead of Him."

Cavanagh sighed once more. She knew that Cleary was correct in his words. She just didn't have to like them. She looked around as she heard footsteps and stared at Simon who stopped in the doorway. He had come to find her. He just had not expected to find her in Cleary's arms. Blackie was correct, he decided. These two were a couple whether they acknowledged it or not.

"Simon? I didn't expect you to come so soon." Cavanagh didn't move. She felt safe in his arms. "Cleary? This is Simon Gardiner. His wife is Eavan, pronounced Eve-een. He works with Blackie, I think we told you."

"You did. Nice to meet you, Simon. Now, are we just going to stand here staring at one another or are we heading for Cavanagh's?" Cleary's grin widened as Cavanagh elbowed him.

"I would think so, Cavanagh. We've picked up some food for us, just cold stuff and sandwiches and that kind of stuff." Simon grinned and disappeared from view.

Cavanagh and Cleary didn't move, neither one wanting to. They eventually headed back outside for their cars and headed for her home. Cavanagh was not sure what to expect but she knew that the meeting would change things for her. All she could do was pray that this would be over and over soon.

Chapter 24

Cavanagh paused as she reached for plates. She was uncertain as to why Simon had appeared. She knew that he had received the emails that she had sent. Cavanagh just had not expected Simon and Eavan to appear.

"Cavanagh?" Eavan's soft voice held a hint of an accent. She had been adopted as a baby when her mother had abandoned her and raised by Irish parents and her paternal Irish grandmother.

"Eavan? What do I do? How do I keep Cleary safe?" Cavanagh struggled to control her emotions.

Eavan reached to hug her, her eyes on Cleary as he stood nearby. She nodded to herself. There was interest there, she could see. She relived her first days of learning her feelings for Simon and remembered how hard it had been.

"It's not up to you, Cavanagh. That's something that is really hard to understand and accept. Your lives are in God's hands. He has ultimate control over what happens to you. You know our story, how both Simon and I almost died. God allowed that. You also know the stories of Jacob, Blackie, and Josh."

"I do. It's different, though, when you're the one going through it. It's much harder to see God's hand working it all out." Cavanagh stepped backwards and into Cleary who simply wrapped her into his arms. "Cleary?"

“Cavanagh? Eavan is corrected. I’ve talked to Blackie and heard their stories. We’re not safe and we don’t know when we will be. We’re working on it. So is Will.” Cleary was frustrated at that. He wanted it all over so that he could date Cavanagh. He paused, knowing that he wouldn’t be waiting for that.

An hour later, the group looked around at one another. Cavanagh rose to clear the table, Eavan and Foley helping her. Dagen had risen and retrieved the material. He watched his granddaughter carefully, seeing the edginess that was there and that was not her.

Cleary shoved Cavanagh back into her chair and then sat beside her. His eyes were on Simon who was watching them both closely. He nodded. Simon had an idea, Cleary decided, and that might just solve this.

Will appeared at that point, coming in as a friend only. He was off duty and had been worried about both Cleary and Cavanagh. He took with thanks the pate of food handed to him. It had been a busy day for him and he had not had time to grab even a quick sandwich.

Simon glanced down at his notes. He wasn’t sure now that this was a good idea. He felt Eavan’s arm around him as she leaned into him.

“Simon? What do you have?” Foley spoke for the others, his eyes on his daughter. She was stressed almost beyond what she could handle.

“I’m not quite sure, Foley. Let’s go through it and see what we can come up with. I know someone who I can reach out to if that is what you want to do.” Simon prayed for his friends. He knew that this was not over by a long shot. "So, Webster? He's still in town?"

Will nodded. Webster was hiding on them, knowing that he was wanted for abducting Cavanagh.

"We're actively looking for him but he's in hiding. Until we find him, Cavanagh is still at great risk." Will drew a deep breath. "Cavanagh, we need to keep you safe and that will be difficult given your work. Cleary, the same goes for you. You will be targeted just because of your relationship with Cavanagh. Foley and Dagen. The same for you. You are not safe just because."

"We understand that, Will. Now, what about this?" Dagen lifted a corner of the paperwork in front of him. "How does that help us get ahead of them?"

"That we can discuss. First, let's spend time in prayer." Simon simply bowed his head and prayed with the others following after him. He looked up when they finished, a thoughtful look on his face. "Cavanagh, talk to me. Tell me what you were thinking when you were searching."

Cavanagh shrugged, her thoughts muddled for a moment, totally unlike her.

"I'm not really sure, Simon. You know me. I usually am very organized with my thoughts. This time, they seemed to be all over the place. I would have an idea and then another and another. I had to keep writing down each idea. God seemed to be guiding me. Why?"

"Because you have found newspaper articles that I am not sure that we would even have thought to look for. And obituaries and birth notices. God was leading you. You have the foundations of a family tree for Webster, did you know that?" Simon grinned at her.

"No, I didn't realize that I did. How did I do that?" Cavanagh flipped through her papers.

"You do have that. I would like to pass it on to a lady who can help us. But for now, let's work through what you have. Living in this town all your life helps. You know the people as do your dad and granddad."

"That we do, Simon." Dagen spoke up, having read through what Cavanagh had found. "Cavanagh has found just about everything that is public knowledge on Webster. It's the private information that you don't have. And that I can tell you some of it as can Foley." Dagen went on to describe what he knew and who Webster's contacts were. He could see Will jotting them down.

"Dagen? This last name? That woman? How is she connected to Webster?" Will frowned at his notes.

"That's his half-sister. They hide it and always have." Foley spoke up. "She's around my age, Webster a couple of years younger."

Will was nodding at that. He had work to do on this investigation but he also had other investigations to work on. He rose at last, exhausted mentally, and headed home. He didn't see the vehicle that followed him and then parked outside of his house. A friend was watching out for him.

Cavanagh tidied up her home and then headed for her office. She stood and stared down at the pile of paperwork. She felt as if they had moved their case along as it was said but she wasn't quite sure if that had really happened. Cleary had hugged her as he left and dropped a kiss on her cheek. She had stood fo ages afterwards with a hand on her cheek, wonder in her eyes. Cavanagh wasn't sure what that meant but it gave hope to her, hope that just maybe Cleary returned the feelings that she was beginning to have. She finally turned and retired, knowing that she had to be up for work in the morning.

Cleary stared at the clock. It was three in the morning and he had not slept, not one wink. He was deeply worried about his lady as he had become to think of Cavanagh. His mind was just too active to sleep. He sighed and shoved back the blankets. Reaching for clean clothes, he dressed and then headed to make a pot of coffee. He was going to need it.

With a mug of coffee in his hand, Cleary headed for his office. He reached for his work orders and sorted through them before he set them to one side. Even though his leg had healed, there were days when it ached. He was grateful for Jeff's help. He was glad to pass on the knowledge that he had acquired over the years, knowledge that could only be acquired from actual experience at work.

Cleary reached for his Bible instead of the pile of papers that he had dropped on the desk the night before. He wanted to go through them but he knew that he needed to spend time in prayer and Bible study. His head bowed over the Book that he loved. He didn't hear the soft noise outside of his house. He rose at last, heading for the kitchen and his breakfast. His phone was out as he sent a good morning text to his lady, smiling at her prompt reply.

Chapter 25

A week or so later, Cleary walked back towards his work truck, watching as Jeff was tucking away the equipment that they had used. He was grateful for Jeff's help. There were days, such as that day, when walking and working on uneven ground taxed his strength to its utmost. His leg was paining that day.

Jeff turned as he felt Cleary beside him, a frown on his face for a moment.

"We're done for the day?" It was only mid-afternoon on a Friday. He thought for sure that Cleary would move on to another site to survey but he saw the pain and fatigue on Cleary's face.

"Not today, Jeff. We're packing in early. We didn't take time for lunch so I'm treating you to a meal." Cleary locked the back of the truck and then headed for the driver's side. He paused before he keyed the motor to life. "Where do you want to eat, Jeff?"

Jeff shrugged. He had learned quickly that Cleary had a soft heart and cared deeply for his friends. Cleary considered Jeff and his family his friends.

"I don't know. A burger?" Jeff grinned as Cleary shook his head. This was usual for them on a Friday, to share a late lunch before they headed into the weekend. He didn't feel as if he was working but he knew that he was. He was also learning a lot from Cleary, who didn't hesitate to explain his actions to Jeff and who also lent him books to read. Jeff was thankful for the compassion and caring that Cleary showed.

Cleary pulled into a popular diner where he felt they served the best hamburgers. He felt Jeff's finger poke his arm.

"Cavanagh's here. She's walking across to the diner." Jeff had spied Cavanagh, not sure if Cleary had spotted her or not.

"She is?" Cleary quickly parked and then was almost running across the parking lot, Jeff trailing after him. "Cavanagh? You're just getting your lunch?"

Cavanagh spun, fear briefly showing on her face, before she relaxed. She had been on edge all that day, feeling as if she had been followed as she had been out and about. She was glad that she had finished the work that she had to do and was heading back to the shop to grab her car and head home.

"Cleary? Aren't you working?" She walked into his hug, feeling safe for the first time that day.

"We're done for the day. We didn't take time for lunch. What about you?" Cleary hung her around to head into the diner, Jeff on her other side.

"I'm done as well. It was a busy day and I didn't take time to eat." Cavanagh slid onto a bench seat in a booth and found Cleary beside her, a grin on his face. Jeff slid in on the opposite side, a grin on his own face.

Finishing their meal, the three made their way out of the diner, heading for their vehicle. Both Cavanagh and Cleary had work to do to finish off before the weekend and when they could set aside their duties for the weekend. Cleary had already asked Cavanagh to spend Saturday with him, doing something fun. He hadn't shared his plans with her.

The next morning, Cleary walked towards Cavanagh's house, finding Cavanagh on the front porch waiting for him. He simply swept her into a hug with a prayer murmured in her ear. Cavanagh was gradually relaxing around Cleary, knowing that he would not harm her. In fact, she was certain that he would give his life to protect her. And that she was so afraid that was what would happen.

Cleary stared down at her, his thoughts muddled and troubled. He had made plans to take her on a hike that day with a picnic lunch already in his backpack. Now, he wasn't sure that the hike was such a good idea after all.

"Cleary?" Cavanagh's hesitant question had him shaking his head before he dropped a kiss on her cheek. "What are we up to today?"

"I thought a hike and a picnic. I'm now not sure if that's a good idea." Cleary bit at his lip, watching her process his words.

"I refuse to hide any more, Cleary. I intend to live my life and be out and about. You can do what you want."

"I'm going to be out there with you." Cleary hesitated for a moment, praying that he was not overstepping the boundaries of their friendship. "I want to date you, Cavanagh. I have never wanted to date before. You are a beautiful, special, compassionate lady that I don't want to lose from my life."

Cavanagh stared up at him, wondering at his height, before she just hugged him.

"I want that too, Cleary. I thought that I would have to ask you out on a date." Cavanagh hugged him once more before he was running with her to tuck her into his truck.

Three hours later, Cleary paused by a stream, his arm around Cavanagh. They had found the local conservation area and had hiked for a while. It was nearing lunch time and Cleary had paused at a favourite picnic area of his.

"This is where I like to eat, Cavanagh. Does it suit?" Cleary grinned at her.

"It does. It's one of my favourite spots as well. I come here sometimes just to find peace and commune with God without all the distractions of our modern life. I equate it as spending time in the garden with Christ." She blinked for a moment, having just shared one of her deepest feelings.

"I like that thought. And I like the thought of being prayed for in the Garden all those years ago. God cares about us and has our story already set."

"He does at that." Cavanagh knelt by the stream, a hand in the cold water. "Cleary? What is your take on all of this that we're going through?"

"My take on this?" Cleary's hands paused as he was setting out their meal on the blanket that he had already spread out. "I'm not sure, Cavanagh. I know that it is driving me deeper into the Bible and having me spend more time in prayer. Was that the reason? It is part of it. I just don't have a sense of what is really the reason for this or who's behind it." He glanced up as she sat near him. "What about you?"

Cavanagh shrugged. Her thoughts were troubled. She had thought about the why's for far too long.

"I think we're being used to bring someone to justice. It goes beyond Webster. I am afraid that he will kidnap me again. He meant harm to come to me. He just didn't say what he had in mind. How do we take him down?"

Cleary grinned at her words before he bit into his sandwich and chewed thoughtfully. He nodded at last. That was his fear, that Webster would walk in and make Cavanagh disappear.

"I think that you are correct in that. He has people watching us and watching your dad and granddad. Now, let's set this aside for now. We'll talk about it, sweetheart. I promise you that."

Their meal finished, the two sat in silence, the sounds of the forest and stream soothing their spirits. On their feet at last, they headed back towards Cleary's truck. A sound in front of him had Cleary pausing and then drawing Cavanagh off of the trail and into hiding in the undergrowth.

Three men walked rapidly past them. They were obviously not hikers. Cleary changed a worried look with Cavanagh before he was out on the trail again and running for his truck. Cavanagh kept pace with him, her head slightly turned to watch behind them. Cleary shoved her into his truck and took off before he fastened his seatbelt. Cavanagh reached to help him do that.

Reaching the town limits, Cleary slowed and then pulled into a busy parking lot. He then stopped in a parking spot, his eyes on the rearview mirror. He drew in a deep breath of relief. They were safe, for now, but he had no idea how long that would be for.

Cavanagh stared at him, shock on her face. She couldn't believe that they had just done that.

"Cleary? Were they after us?"

"It's possible." Cleary continued to search the area around them, worried that they had been followed after all. "They weren't out there just for a hike. They were on a mission, as Jeff would say."

"They were. And I think that they were after us." Cavanagh slumped back against the seat, a troubled look on her face.

"They were. And I want to know why." Cleary took a look at his watch. "There's a lady who lives about an hour from here. I know her husband. Why don't we head that way and talk to her? She has a business that finds people. I'm sure that she's already working on this if word has reached her." He groaned as his phone chimed. He pulled it out, frowning at it before he grinned. "She's in our town right now, in fact, sitting outside of my house. "Let's go find her/"

"She does that?" Cavanagh was surprised but she knew from Blackie that was what they did.

"She does. Her husband has a security team. He'll give us some ideas on how to stay safe." Cleary drove away, heading for his house, watchful for anyone tailing them.

Chapter 26

Cavanagh studied the couple that Cleary was greeting. She looked down as she felt a tap on her leg and found a little fellow with his arms stretched up for her to pick him up. She grinned at his grin and did just that. She was surprised at the tight hug that she received and then all the kisses that covered her face. She was laughing as the lady gave an exclamation and came towards her.

"Isaac!" Emma Finlay reached for her son who simply tightened his hold on Cavanagh all the while grinning at his mother.

"It's okay. Really it is. He's so sweet." Cavanagh reached out a hand to shake Emma's. "I'm Cavanagh."

"And I am Emma Finlay. This is our son, Isaac. He usually doesn't do this so quickly. He at least waits for five or ten minutes." Emma's grin lit up her face. "You're special, he's telling me."

"And so is he." Cavanagh continued to grin as Cleary approached.

"Cavanagh? This is Abe. He tells me as well that his son is acting out of character, at least to some extent." Cleary was delighted at the reception that Cavanagh had been given.

"He's adorable." Cavanagh tilted her head towards the house. "We are going in, aren't we?"

Cleary laughed as he headed towards the house, unlocking the door and disengaging the security system. He noted Abe taking a look at it before he nodded. Joseph, one of Abe's men, had set it up for him and he was grateful for that.

"Cavanagh?" Emma reached to take Isaac from her despite his protests. "How are you really doing?"

Cavanagh shrugged. She was not sure what to say. She really didn't know herself how she was.

"To tell you the truth? I'm not sure. I'm out and about, working as I need to. I just worry about Cleary and Dad and Grand." Cavanagh's face grew sober.

"That is a worry. And they worry about you in return. How do we help you?" Emma shared a look with Abe. She had been finding information that needed to be shared with the two in front of her. She just wasn't sure how that would go over.

"I don't know, Emma. I really don't. I don't get a sense that I am being followed but they just seemed to turn up wherever we are." Cavanagh didn't hear Abe walking from the house without even reaching for his jacket, Cleary trailing after him.

"Abe?" Cleary watched as Abe searched his vehicle.

"Cleary? They have trackers on your vehicle. I need to search Cavanagh's before I leave and also her family's as well. Work vehicles will need that to." Abe held up a bag with trackers in them. "We need to get these to your investigator."

“And we will.” Cleary sighed. “That’s why we have not been receiving anything, correct?”

“More than likely. You’ll need to lock your truck away when you can. I’ll show you what to watch for.” Abe’s eyes lifted to the porch where Cavanagh stood watching them. “I’ll need to show Cavanagh as well.”

Cleary gave a slight smile. He agreed with Abe. Cavanagh would insist on being told what had been found.

“You will, Abe. She will insist on that.” Cleary walked back up the steps, wrapping Cavanagh in his arms. “He found tracking devices, Cavanagh.”

“I’ve been searching my vehicles, the work van, and the others. I haven’t found any as yet.” Cavanagh shared a look with Abe. “Will made sure that I knew what to look for.”

“That’s good. Now, let’s get back inside and see what Emma has to tell us.” Abe turned and glanced around. He could feel evil around the house and hesitated before he walked back down the steps and searched around the house and the garage as well as the garden shed. He didn’t find anything that he shouldn’t have found. That puzzled him. He had fully expected to find tech objects around the house or in the gardens. Abe walked back into the house, lost in thought.

Emma had reached for the material that she had set to one side. They had gathered in Cleary’s office, Cavanagh bringing in a tray of sweets and coffee for the three of them and tea for Emma.

"Cavanagh? Cleary? This is heavy stuff that we need to go through. Let us pray with you first. It's what we always do. And before you ask, Cavanagh, we have gone through stuff such as you are as have all of our team members and many friends." Emma shared a look with Abe.

Thirty minutes passed as they petitioned the heavens for protection for the couple and for answers. Emma handed over the material when they had finished, Cavanagh sitting tight to Cleary. He glanced down at her, seeing the fear in her eyes that she would not allow on her face.

"What did you find, Emma? And explain what it is that you actually do." Cleary grinned at Abe as the other man shook his head.

Emma nodded, knowing that she had to explain. She told Cavanagh that she ran a business where she located people, places, and other information. She could not explain how she did it. It was how her brain worked. Her investigative business was beginning to expand as she brought in remote workers who were friends that they had helped.

"This is what we have found, Cavanagh. You two read it through and then we'll talk." Emma kept watching them and saw as they found information and were making notes. She nodded. This is what she had expected from Cleary, a friend who had moved from Riverville to this town.

Abe was on his feet at one point, moving away to take a phone call. His voice was quiet as he asked questions before he pocketed his phone and then paced the foyer of the house. He had been given information from his business partner, Murphy, that he needed to give to those two.

Chapter 27

Cavanagh paced through her home the next afternoon. She had sent Cleary home even though she hadn't wanted to. Her father and grandfather had sat beside the couple in church and then headed out on their own activities. Cavanagh was feeling smothered and she knew why. The men in her life were trying to take care of her and protect her. She just didn't think that it would work. Someone was outside her home who wanted to harm her. Cavanagh had felt them moving in bit by bit.

Her prayers were becoming more frantic, she decided, as she begged God to protect her and bring an end to this. She just didn't know if that would happen and she would live or if she would die. She just prayed that the men in her life survived.

Cavanagh picked up the paperwork that she had just dropped on the desk in her office the day before. She had not been surprised at who Emma had discovered. She knew that person only too well and knew that they kept themselves hidden in the background of the town. Cavanagh had always felt the undercurrents that ran through her town. She had spent time discussing them with Foley and Dagen. Neither man could explain why it was that person was who they were. They simply stated that they had always had a hidden side to them.

Cleary had walked away reluctantly from Cavanagh that afternoon. He had wanted to stay with her and protect her from the unseen danger that was swelling around her. All he could do was be there when she would allow him and smother her in prayer at other times. He had spent the night pouring over the information that Emma had let, not sleeping the night before. Cleary yawned before he stretched out on the couch. He set the alarm on his watch for an hour, knowing that would be enough sleep to get him through the rest of the day.

Dagen rose from where he had been sitting, Foley seated nearby. The two men had spent time in prayer for their girl and her guy as Foley called him. They were deeply worried but knew that God was watching out for them. Dagen was puzzled by what Emma had left them. He knew the reputation of her company, Trackers, but had never thought that she would be investigating his granddaughter.

Foley was deep in thought. He knew all of the individuals that Cavanagh had discovered and also the ones that Emma had named. It frightened him to some extent. He had reached out to Will, asking Will to call him in the morning. It could wait until then. Will had been puzzled when Foley had called but had agreed to call in the morning. This would set off a deeper investigation, Foley knew. He just didn't know if everyone named would be involved or not. They had to cast a wide net that much he knew.

On the move the next morning, Cavanagh simply went from job site to job site. It was a busy morning before she headed back to the work shop. Foley was waiting for her, reaching to hug his daughter.

"Have a good day?"

"I did, Dad. How about you?" Cavanagh's eyes narrowed as he grinned at her. "What are you up to?"

"Absolutely nothing. It's Dad who is." Foley grinned at his father. "He's planning on a meal tonight with Cleary, Will, and Jeff and his family if they will join us."

"Oh, that sounds wonderful." Cavanagh hugged her father and then her grandfather. "What time?"

"We're closing up now, Cavanagh." Dagen grinned at her in turn. "Head off and get cleaned up. We're meeting at my place."

Cleary watched as Jeff and his parents interacted with Dagen. He could tell that they were acquainted with one another. His head turned as Foley stopped beside him.

"Cleary? How are you holding up?" Foley was worried about his young friend.

Cleary shrugged. He had no idea how to feel. He was asked that almost on a daily basis.

"I'm not sure, Foley. It's hard to know how to respond to that question."

"It is." Foley watched Will as he watched Cleary. "Has Will said anything?"

Cleary shook his head. Will had not said anything, and that troubled Cleary. He wanted this over with and over that day.

"He hasn't said anything yet. I know that Emma has been in touch with him. That's what she said she would do."

"I'm glad. We need to go over what she found." Foley watched Cleary. Cleary was wearing out, Foley decided. He could see the pain that he was trying to hide.

"We do. I just don't know what to say, though. You know the town. What are your thoughts?" Cleary watched Foley for a moment before his gaze shifted to Will. He was slightly discomforted to find Will studying him intently. He walked away, an arm coming around Cavanagh who leaned into his hug. It was obvious to all of them that the two were a couple.

Dagen stared out of his living room window after everyone had left. He had turned out all the lights and simply stared up at the stars in the night sky. It was coming up to the Christmas season. He wanted this over for his granddaughter before that. He begged God for that to happen. Dagen frowned for a moment, thinking back over the meal that had been shared. It had been a time to relax and forget about what was happening. He felt that they had been able to do that. Dagen was glad that he had followed the nudge that God had given him to plan the meal.

He turned for the window and stared around the darkness of his living room before he headed for his office. He sat heavily in his desk chair, his head buried in his hands. He didn't know what to do other than to pray.

Cavanagh snuggled down under the blankets, her eyes closing as she thought through the day and then through what Emma had told them. She was frustrated to say the least. She wanted this over but it didn't seem that it would be at any time soon.

Her eyes popped open for a moment before she reached for the pad of paper and pen to jot down notes. She set aside the paper and pen and slept. She didn't know that the next few weeks would bring more danger to all of them.

Chapter 28

Cleary stared at the Lockyer house, trying to determine just what the problem was with it. He had done his research but nothing could be found that explained why it was abandoned. He walked around the house, studying it and then studying the land around it. He was still puzzled by the request to survey the property, just as if it had been put up for sale.

Turning to lean against his truck, Cleary frowned. There was something off about the whole thing, he knew. He just couldn't figure out what. His head turned as he heard a vehicle.

Will shut the door of his car and stood for a moment, his eyes closing as he sought an answer for all this. He walked towards Cleary, turning to lean against the truck as well.

"Cleary?" Will waited patiently for Cleary to speak.

"Will? What is it about this house or this property? It doesn't make sense that Cavanagh and I were called out here. I looked through all the record that I could find. There is nothing to show that the property has been sold. There is nothing to show that it has gone through probate. The taxes are still being paid through a trust fund. So why?" Cleary didn't look at Will. He didn't want to see censure on that man's face at the questions that he was asking and yet not asking.

"I know, Cleary. It doesn't make any sense at al. What brought you out here today?" Will again waited for Cleary together his thoughts and speak.

Cleary shrugged. He had no idea why he had come out there. Something inside him had led him to that point.

"I don't know, Will. It's not the first time that I've walked around this house or around the edge of the property. I want this over for Cavanagh and her family. They don't deserve to be living in fear all the time."

"No one does, Cleary. We want this over for them as well. We're just missing that one piece of information that would do that." Will was frustrated at that. "Talk to me. Tell me what you are thinking and feeling. Sometimes, it just one little thing that helps to solve a crime. And yes, this is a crime against you two."

Cleary nodded. It was a crime. This is when he wished that he had family that he could turn to. Only he didn't have that. Cavanagh was becoming that to him. Foley and Dagen had taken him in as a son and grandson.

"I don't know where to start." Cleary blinked for a moment against the tears that welled up in his eyes. He was not afraid to cry. This was jut not the time to do so.

"I don't know where to start, Will. We have talked this over so many times. You know my life up until I moved here. I think that you have picked my brain clean."

Will's hand on his arm stopped him. A thought had crossed his mind.

"Why did you move here, Cleary? You could have set up anywhere."

"I know. I just liked this town and area. The surveyor who lived here was retiring. I spoke with him and he helped me to set up my business." Cleary paled at that. "Was I set up?"

Will stared at him. He had not thought about that. He had been remiss in that.

"Unfortunately, we can't speak with him. He died from a heart attack just before you moved here. You wouldn't have known that. You were busy setting up your business and taking in clients. His death was not suspicious, not that we know of. He had had a heart attack a couple of years before that." Will knew that he would need to dig into that information now. His work had just increased. "Come on, Cleary. Let's get you home. You've been out working today."

"I have been, Will. And I do need to get home. I'm taking Cavanagh out for a meal and she'll be waiting for me." Cleary took one more look at the house, feeling watched and not seeing anyone who was doing that.

Cavanagh watched Cleary closely early that evening. They were sitting in a local restaurant that they both liked. She frowned at him and found him smiling at her.

"Cleary? What did you do?" Cavanagh continued to frown at him.

"Nothing. I was talking with Will early. He asked me why I chose this town." Cleary and Cavanagh had talked about that.

"He had never asked you that?" Cavanagh's hand rested on Cleary's hand. "I would have thought that he would have done that."

"He hadn't. I have no connection to this town from before. He told me that the surveyor who was here had died."

"He did. He was well liked in town and in the surrounding areas. He was like you. He would take youths under his wing and train then, just as you are doing. They would sometimes go on to take up surveying or go on to something else. His funeral took a long time just because of so many who wanted to tell what he had done for them." Cavanagh blinked as she remembered that.

"He did? I guess that I'm following in his footsteps, then. Jeff is so eager to learn." Cleary's hands were on the table, palm up. He waited for Cavanagh to study him and then study his hands before she placed hers into his. He smiled at her, knowing that she was still not sure if she was doing what she really wanted to. "Cavanagh? You do the same. I've seen you working and talking with the youth at the church. You didn't know that. I kept in the background, just observing. I didn't feel as if I could speak with you."

"I know. I saw you. I wanted you to come forward and work with the youth. They were waiting for you to do that."

“They were?” Cleary saw Cavanagh nod. “I guess then that I should. But that leaves you and me.”

“You and me? I’m not sure what you mean. I know that you said that you wanted to date.” Cavanagh waited for Cleary to speak.

“I do, Cavanagh. I really do. You’re a beautiful, compassionate lady who models Christ’s teachings so well. I want to date with an idea of seeing where we go. Does that work for you?”

Cleary stared at him. This had been her thought as well. Only she thought that she was too dangerous for that to happen. She nodded, feeling Cleary’s hands tighten on her.

“You have to get past Dad and Granddad, but I think that you already have done that.” Cavanagh smiled at him, guessing correctly that he had already spoken to the men in her life.

Chapter 29

Cleary paused in his work a few days later. He frowned at the pole that Jeff was holding for him before he shook his head. His mind was not on his work that day and it needed to be. He struggled to complete what he had to do that day before packing everything away for the day.

Jeff opened his mouth to say something and then snapped it closed. He studied the area around him, feeling them being watched but he could not see anyone. He turned to Cleary, finding Cleary staring around as well.

"Cleary? What's going on?" Jeff hesitated before he asked his boss what was going on.

"I don't know, Jeff. We need to get out of here." Cleary moved quickly to slide behind the wheel and drive away. He didn't see the car that pulled out after him and then followed him through town to his office building.

Jeff was away with a wave, heading for his father's car. He searched the area once more, not comfortable about leaving Cleary on his own.

Cleary tidied away what he had been using, organizing the back of his truck. He kept pausing, his eyes rising to search the area around him. Cleary knew that someone was watching him. He just couldn't see whoever it was.

Walking up to his front door an hour later, Cleary's steps paused. His eyes closed for a moment before they opened and he stared at the house. Something seemed off that day and Cleary just wasn't sure what it was. He dropped his briefcase and lunch bag on the back porch and then stalked around his house, watching for anything out of the ordinary.

Cleary paused as he walked up the front steps, a frown on his face. He stared down at the old rusty skeleton keys that lay in front of him. The keys were tied together by a dirty old string. Cleary shook his head, not sure what they meant, before he reached to pick them up. He fingered each one, turning them over and over in his hand. He had no idea who would have left them but he knew someone who could help him to decide what they would unlock.

Listening as Cleary explained how he had found the keys, Cavanagh walked back towards her kitchen. She had been surprised to find Cleary at her door, not having planned on seeing him that day.

"Cleary? Slow down. What are you talking about?" Cavanagh set down another bowl of soup on the table and reached to make another grilled cheese sandwich even as she pointed at Cleary to sit.

"I found these on my front porch. Old skeleton keys. I have no idea who left them or why. What can you tell me about them?" Cleary was agitated, that much was obvious. He wanted to know what locks these keys belonged to.

Cavanagh reached for them and then set them to one side. She frowned at Cleary as he glared at her.

"We eat first, Cleary, and then we try and determine what is going on. You haven't had your supper, I don't think. I'm starved. I will not look at them until we have eaten." Cavanagh bowed her head to pray, knowing full well that Cleary was not happy with her words.

Rising to help clear away the table, Cleary paused at the keys, a finger out to touch them. A thought crossed his mind that horrified him. He turned to find Cavanagh standing beside him and simply wrapped her into a tight hug. She clung to him, drawing comfort from his strength.

"We need to pray, Cleary." Her voice was muffled against him.

"We do, Cavanagh." He spun her around and headed for her office, the keys snatched from the table. "Let's work in here, if you don't mind."

Cavanagh stared at him as he shoved her down into a chair and then found the one right next to hers. Her hand was tight in his as he bowed his head and begged for protection for his lady. He didn't realize that was how he had prayed but Cavanagh heard each word and wondered at them in her heart.

His head raised at last, Cleary once more stared at the keys in his hands. He felt Cavanagh's fingers lightly brush his as she reached for the keys.

Cavanagh frowned at them. She was puzzled about why Cleary would have received any keys. If it had been her that had received them, it would have made sense. A sudden chill chased down her spine and she shuddered from it.

"Cleary? Where did you find these again?"

"On my front porch when I came home. I checked my security feed. It didn't show anyone leaving them there but I would need someone to check to ensure that the feed had not been tampered with." He rubbed at the back of his neck. "What are you thinking?"

"That these belong to the Lockyer house. And they are trying to draw us back there to go into it again. Only this time, we won't come out. I fear that is what the plan is." Cavanagh's face was white as she spoke, fear evident on it.

"I see. That was my question. How do we know for sure?" Cleary was on his feet to pace. His thoughts were troubled and he found it difficult to pray. Cleary knew that this was a circumstance in which the Holy Spirit would pray for him.

"We need to talk to Will." Cavanagh was on her feet, heading for the kitchen where she had left her phone. She sent a quick text message off to Will, who read it and then frowned. The appearance of the keys puzzled him as well. He simply responded that he would drop by in about an hour. Would the two of them please stay safe?

Cleary reached for the keys, studying them. They were rusty but there seemed to be something about them that drew him to take a closer look.

"Cleary? What are you thinking?" Cavanagh stood in front of him, her arms wrapped around herself. She too was puzzled by the keys.

"I'm not sure what to think, Cavanagh. This means danger for us, that's a given. I just don't know why we would have them."

"I think you're right. They belong to the Lockyer place. But skeleton keys can open up a variety of doors. That's why they have that name. Will said he'd drop by."

"He can look at them but I'm not turning them over to him." Cleary was adamant about that.

"And we're not exploring that Lockyer house. It's too dangerous for us to go in. Not unless we have a police escort." Cavanagh walked away to answer the door, frowning at Will as he stepped inside.

"Cavanagh?" Will wasn't sure what to say, given the look on her face that he just could not read.

"Those keys? They likely belong to the Lockyer house. Cleary wants to investigate." Cavanagh walked away, Will following her.

Chapter 30

Will reached for the keys, taking them from Cleary's hand. He too was puzzled that Cleary had received the keys. He would have thought that Cavanagh would have been the one to do that. He studied them, turning them over and over just as Cleary had done.

"Cavanagh? Does anything strike you as odd about these keys?" Will looked up to find her studying the keys as well.

Cavanagh shrugged. She could not think of what was bothering her about the keys, other than that they had been dropped on Cleary's porch.

"I don't know, Will. I don't see anything on them that is triggering any ideas. Cleary thinks that they belong to the Lockyer house. They might. But then again skeleton keys can be used to open up any lock that takes them. There are difference in the keys but one will open more than one lock." Cavanagh backed slightly away, feeling fear welling up inside her. "I don't like them, Will. What do you want to do about them?"

Will grinned at Cavanagh, knowing that she was scared and worried but was also wanting to go on the offensive. He would see what he could do about that.

"I really don't know, Cavanagh. There is no hint at all as to where they go or what locks that they will open." Will stood for a few moments, lost in thought. He knew that he would have to head for the Lockyer house at some point. And that meant that he had to have a locksmith with him. That meant one of the O'Rourkes would likely need to be with him. "I'll need to head that way." He shared a look with Cleary. He knew right well that Cleary would be right there with them.

"Okay, then. Saturday?" Cavanagh knew that she was booked up for the next few days. Cleary was as well, he had said.

"Saturday it is, then." Will finally walked away, not sure that he was doing the right thing. He had left the keys with Cleary. He had no reason to take them into evidence as yet. They had been left for Cleary.

Saturday found the three of them standing in the driveway at the Lockyer house. They stared at each other and then at the house. Cavanagh finally sighed and moved that way, stepping carefully up onto the porch. She froze as her thoughts reverted to the accident or whatever it had been weeks ago. She wasn't sure if she could enter the house but she needed to for Cleary's sake and yes, for her own sake as well.

Cleary reached for Cavanagh's hand as he approached her. He didn't have to ask to know how scared she was. He was as well. He tugged her with him along the wraparound porch and then stopped at a side door. Cleary looked at Will who gave a slight nod before Cavanagh reached to unlock the door. She had to search for the right key which had not surprised her. The door squeaked open and then stopped as if it had hit something behind it.

Will moved to walk through the door first, stepping carefully. He held his breath for a moment, waiting for the floor to collapse under him. Cavanagh and Cleary followed slowly, Cavanagh's hand clinging tightly to Cleary.

"Where do we look?" Cleary's voice sounded loud in the room, which seemed to be a library. He looked around at the dust and debris and felt sad that the room had come to that. The broken windows had let in the elements and there was destruction in the room from that.

"I don't know, Cleary. It would have been nice if they had left instructions with the keys. But they didn't." Will looked around, stopping abruptly as he ran into a spider web. He brushed it from his face and hair, hearing Cavanagh giggling behind him. "It's not funny, Cavanagh." His voice had a hint of his own laughter in it.

"I know. It's just nerves, I think." Cavanagh moved around the room. "There has to be something hidden here." She touched the book shelves, a frown on her face. "I don't think that these move away from the wall." She stared around and then walked out of the room, leaving the two men to stare at one another before they moved rapidly after her.

Will's hand reached out to stop her. He could feel the evil in the house and wanted them out of there. Cavanagh shrugged off his hand, continuing to explore the main floor of the house. Cleary stood and studied the grand stairs that rose to the second floor. He wanted to climb them but didn't trust that they would be safe.

Will too stared at the steps before he cautiously walked up them. Cavanagh gave a shrug at the look that Cleary shot her way before she followed Will. Cleary sighed and his head dropped for a moment. Cavanagh was not letting him do what he needed to do and that was to protect her. All he could do was pray for protection for them all. He just wasn't sure if that would happen.

Cavanagh paused in the hallway, her eyes on the rooms that she had just entered and exited. There was nothing there that could lead them to any answers. She walked towards a narrow and dark stairway that lay at the end of the hallway. Her eyes sought the door that was at the top of the stairs and she shuddered. Fear was growing inside her even as she climbed the steps. Will was behind her, reaching past her to try the door. They shared a look as it too swung open, hitting hard against the wall behind it.

Will moved past Cavanagh to stand just inside the door of the attic. He looked around, surprised to see that the room was empty. It was not what he had expected. He motioned for Cavanagh and Cleary to stay where they were standing and walked around the area himself. Will frowned. There was nothing there that anything was amiss or off. Yet, he could feel the evil in the house. He pointed back down the stairs and followed the two ahead of him at a rapid pace.

The trio chose the stairs that led to the kitchen and then walked out to stand on the grass. They shared a look. That had been a waste of time, they all thought.

Cavanagh looked around, her eyes on the outbuildings before she was heading for what had been the garage at one point. The keys in her hands unlocked the door and she shoved it open, brushing aside dust and debris and cobwebs. She stepped inside, feeling Cleary's hand on her arm.

Cleary looked around, surprised to see no vehicles or anything at all. The building had been stripped clean of anything had been in there. Will followed, a sense of doom filling his thoughts.

A sudden snap and loud crack had them looking around and then running for the door. They just didn't make it in time. The cracking of breaking wood and yells from the men and screams from Cavanagh filled the area before there was silence. The dust and debris settled carefully on the pile of broken lumber that covered the trio.

Chapter 31

Turning away from Cavanagh's back door, Foley frowned. They had planned to share a meal together that Saturday night. Only, his daughter wasn't home and he had no idea where to begin to look for her. Dagen shared a look with him before he was pulling his son with him.

"The Lockyer house, Foley. They had keys that they were heading out to try out on the locks." Dagen's heart was in his throat as he sped that way, not sure if that's where they were but his gut instinct was telling him that they were.

"The Lockyer house? Of course. Cavanagh did mention that. I just pray that they're not harmed." Foley's eyes searched the property through the dimming light as Dagen drove into the driveway. "There's a vehicle here."

"It's Will's. Where are they?" Dagen and Foley were out of the truck almost before it had stopped moving, frantically searching around the house. Dagen returned to his truck to grab the large flashlight, shining it around. A loud cry was wrenched from his body before he was running towards the garage, dismay and fear on his face at the collapse of the building.

"Dad? Are they in there?" Foley froze in his tracks before he was calling for assistance, knowing that he could not get them out. He grabbed his father's keys and ran to move the truck out of the way of the emergency personnel.

Dagen stared in horror at the broken pile of lumber. He could only pray that they were not under that but his heart was telling him that they were. He then began to pray that the three were alive. He could not do anything more than that. Dagen felt Foley's around across his shoulders as they waited for the emergency personnel to appear.

Frantic activity ensued as the firefighters worked to assess the situation. Patrol officers moved the two men back behind Dagen's truck, all the while trying to control their own emotions. Will was a well respected detective who was willing to help anyone who needed it. He was also someone who cared deeply about anyone who approached him.

Dagen leaned against his truck, feeling old. He didn't want to believe that Cavanagh had been hurt once more but that seemed to be the consensus of the emergency workers. He watched closely as a crane was brought in to help remove the debris. Dagen's only prayer was that the three were alive.

Hours seemed to pass but in reality they hadn't. A shout rang out for the paramedics at some point and the men and women ran forward, kits banging along on the stretchers that were pushed towards the wreckage of the garage.

The debris had been carefully moved away from the bodies. Shouts went out that the three were alive. The paramedics and the firefighters worked as rapidly as they could to assess the three and then shift them to the stretchers.

Will was speaking with the emergency personnel, his voice strained and filled with hurt. His eyes closed as the stretcher hits the bumps and hollows in the yard no matter how carefully he was moved.

Dagen and Foley watched him carefully before they crept forward on almost silent feet to be closer to where their girl lay. They watched carefully as Cleary was moved away from the debris, his eyes closed. The two men shared a look as he passed them. He didn't seem to be aware of his surroundings. An investigator approached them.

"Dagen? Foley? We're almost ready to transport Cavanagh. Foley? You're riding with her?" James, the investigator, knew that the two men would be.

"I am. Dad said he'd follow in his truck." Foley frowned at the officer.

"No, we'll drive him there in his truck. That way we can keep up with the ambulance. Head off to get ready. Dagen? John is waiting for you. Hand over your keys." James hesitated and shook his head. "Hand over your keys, Dagen. We'll get your truck to you. Go on with Foley."

Foley almost ran for the ambulance before he spun to wait for the stretcher carrying Cavanagh. Dagen stood with his arm around his son, worried beyond what he could even think that he could bear for Cavanagh. He was also worried about his son.

The wheels on the three stretchers had squeaked and squealed as they had been pushed towards the medical staff waiting for them. The two men were forced to walk away, heading for the waiting room and chairs that would grow to be very uncomfortable over the next while. They had no idea how injured Cavanagh was.

Dagen was on his feet, heading for the clerk. He spoke to her quietly, asking if Foley and himself could be put down as people to be informed about Cleary's condition. She nodded, her fingers tapping away on the keyboard. Dagen had no idea who Cleary's next of kin was but he decided that this needed to be done.

The physicians and other medical staff worked to stabilize the three and then assess them. Diagnostic imaging and blood work were ordered. They were worried about Cavanagh and Cleary, wanting them awake but that wasn't happening as yet.

James walked through the waiting room, searching for Foley and Dagen. He paused before he approached them, handing over the cups of coffee that he held. He sank into a seat beside Dagen, his eyes closing for a moment. It had been a busy, hectic day and this with the three? That had not helped. He had to wait for the garage to be stabilized before he could continue his investigation and that would be into the next day.

"James?" Foley looked around his father, a question on his face.

"Foley? What were they doing out there? I know that Will had gone there on the investigation but why were Cavanagh and Cleary with him?" James had been puzzled at that.

“Cleary found some skeleton keys on his front porch and they decided to see what doors they would unlock at the Lockyer house. I understand that Will spoke with his supervisor about them being there.” Foley was unable to continue, too worried about his daughter.

“That’s what I have been told. They shouldn’t have.” James was angry at the circumstances that had trapped the three, not at the three themselves.

“They had to, James. They need to face what is out there. Hiding isn’t going to solve anything.” Foley’s eyes closed as he prayed for his daughter and their two friends.

Chapter 32

Cleary fought against the hands holding him on the bed. He struggled to rise, his voice worried as he called for Cavanagh. He was deeply afraid that she was dead, even though they told him that she was fine. Cleary dropped back into unconsciousness once more, not realizing that Cavanagh had appeared at his bedside, her hand on his face.

Cavanagh was more worried than she wanted to say. Her father's arm around her kept her on her feet. It was the next day and she had been on her feet since early that morning. She refused to stay in bed, shaking her head when she was told to get back to bed. Cavanagh had asked Will what had happened when she found him in the waiting room.

Will had stared at her for a moment before he informed her that the garage had collapsed on top of them. They had been trapped in a hollow under the debris and that had saved them from any real injury. He knew that Cleary had covered Cavanagh with his own body, saving her from any real harm. Will suspected that Cavanagh was aware of that and that was what was driving her emotions that morning.

Foley's arm tightened around his daughter, his eyes on Cleary. Cleary would not have hesitated at all to protect Cavanagh. He appreciated that but he also worried about Cleary. All he could do at the time was pray for healing for all three of the young people.

Cavanagh turned away at last, heading for the door. Foley still had his arm around her. She stopped as she found Will waiting for her, James at his side.

"Will? James? What is it?" Her face paled even more than it had been.

"We need to talk, Cavanagh." James pointed at the waiting room which was empty at the time. "Sit." He waited for Cavanagh to do just that. "Cavanagh? What did you discover yesterday?"

Cavanagh stared at him, not sure what he was trying to decide.

"Nothing. We found nothing. The garage was empty, which was strange. There should have been things in there. There was nothing there." Cavanagh was worried about that. Her eyes looked towards the hallway and down it towards Cleary's room. She was afraid for him, afraid that next time, he would die and it would be her fault. She couldn't pray. Her prayers didn't seem to be reaching anywhere, she decided.

"What made you go in there?" James had spoken with Will. Will had not had a clear idea as to what Cavanagh had been thinking.

Cavanagh shrugged. She had no clue as to why other than that the keys had to fit a lock somewhere.

"I don't know. I guess that I was just trying out all of the keys. Does that make sense?"

"It does, Cavanagh." Will spoke up at last. He had been removed from the investigation and while he agreed with that, he was disappointed that it had happened. "We couldn't find anything in the house."

Will paused as his phone chimed. Reading the text, his face paled before he looked at James who had pulled out his own phone. "James?"

James nodded before he was on his feet and walked rapidly from the hospital. He drove to the Lockyer house and then dodged the patrol officers and firefighters who milled around. Staring at the house and then the outbuildings, frowning at the smoke that rose from all the buildings. Fire had destroyed every building or pile of debris. What had happened to them? James turned to the arson investigator as he approached him.

"James? How are Will and the others?" Bob was worried about Will. He had seen the pile of debris from the garage that had burned.

"He's on his feet. So is Cavanagh. It's Cleary that's not. He's been awake and fighting to find Cavanagh." James frowned as he stared at the smouldering piles. "What do we have?"

"Arson, plain and simple. Someone poured gasoline all over each of the buildings. As isolated as this place is, it had a good start before it was called in." Bob paused, a horrible thought crossing his mind. "They were set not long after the three were rescued. What if the plan had been to set one of the buildings on fire with them in there?"

James paled at Bob's words. That had not crossed his mind. He drew in a deep breath.

"How do you know that?" James watched as Bob rubbed at his face.

"It's too coincidental, James. They had to have meant that. How did they come to be out here any way?"

"Cleary found a set of skeleton keys on his front porch. They thought that they belonged to here and asked Will to get permission for them to search. From what he said, they had gone through the house and then Cavanagh asked Will to get permission for them to be here. He did and this is the result." James walked away to take his own photos, knowing that he needed them for his investigation. Things had taken a turn that none of them could have expected.

Will studied Cavanagh and saw the exhaustion, pain, and terror in her eyes. She was trying hard to hide it from everyone around her. It wasn't working all that well, he knew. She was on her feet in a few moments and headed for Cleary. Will's head dropped for a moment as he thought through what he knew about the Lockyer house. It was not a lot but what he did know was not pretty.

On his feet, Will walked away, his phone in his hand. He stopped walking, shock on his face, as he read James' text. He spun and walked rapidly back towards where Cavanagh was standing outside of Cleary's room. His arm went around his friend for a moment and Cavanagh leaned against him.

"Will? Why?" Cavanagh's voice held emotions that he had never heard from her before.

"I don't know, Cavanagh. I just heard from James. All the buildings on the Lockyer property were set on fire. I don't think that we were meant to survive." Will's face was still white with shock. Even as a police officer, he had never faced something like this before.

"Arson? They burnt everything?" Cavanagh sighed and then moved the few feet to where Cleary had appeared, his arms around her in a tight hold. "Cleary?"

"I wondered why we were sent there. It makes sick sense, you know? Trap us and then burn the buildings. No one would have known." Cleary felt himself growing angrier by the moment. He knew that he would have to turn that anger over to God. He just wasn't ready to do that at this point.

Chapter. 33

Cleary swayed on his feet, fatigue almost driving him to the floor. Foley had insisted that Cleary stay with him as was Cavanagh. He felt a hand on his shoulder directing him away from the activity in the kitchen and to a bedroom. Cleary was shoved down on the bed and then his feet were raised to the bed, causing him to lie down. He was asleep before he felt the blanket drawn over him.

Foley stood for a moment, his thoughts angry and troubled. It had gone too far now, he decided. He knew that the building had been brought down deliberately onto the three. Foley walked away, heading for where Cavanagh had crashed on the couch. Dagen had covered her with a soft peach blanket before he too had walked away. Foley stood for a moment before he headed for his kitchen, intent on finding Dagen.

Dagen turned to study his son, seeing the anger and fear on his face. He sighed. They were praying for this to end. They were well aware that God was in control. He just wished that God would hurry up and end this. Dagen was afraid, though, of how it would end.

"Dad?" Foley stared at the curtains that covered the window over the sink. "What do we do?"

"I don't know, son. James called. He was checking in to see how our two are. He wants to speak with us sometime tomorrow." Dagen rubbed at his temple, walking to stare down the hallway. His thoughts were with his granddaughter and her fellow. "You and I have to work. Cleary will want to be working, if I know him." Dagen frowned as he heard a sound from Foley.

"Dad?" Foley followed his father, a puzzled look on his face. "What did James say?"

Dagen sighed. He had to be honest with Foley. He just didn't know how to express himself.

"Dad?" Foley repeated his question.

"James did tell me something." Dagen turned to his son. "The building was brought down deliberately. Then at some point after our three were rescued, gasoline was poured all over the buildings and they were set on fire. They would have died, son, if we hadn't found them." Dagen could not continue.

Cavanagh had risen and was now standing behind her grandfather. Horror covered her face for a moment before she spun and almost ran to find Cleary. On her knees beside the bed, her arm wrapped around him. Sobs shook her body and soaked his T-shirt.

Cleary roused, not sure why. He heard Cavanagh's sobs before his arms were around her as he sat up. He gathered her close to him, his own tears trickling down his face. He had no idea why his lady was weeping but he wept with her. He looked up, knowing from the Bible that God bottled their tears. Perhaps at some point, they would understand why they were going through what they were and who was responsible. He prayed that it would be over soon. Cleary just didn't want any more harm to come to his lady. Will had spoken to him earlier that day as had

James. He understood fully what had happened. That scared Cleary. He was ready to gather Cavanagh and her family and run. Except whoever it was would either follow them or wait until they returned.

"Cavanagh? Sweetheart?" Cleary kept his voice low. He looked up as Foley appeared in the doorway and nodded at the older man.

Foley walked away, his heart heavy for his girl. He had not had an easy life, raising Cavanagh on his own for the most part. It had become difficult when she became a teenager and was stretching out, testing her wings. He had been thankful that some of the ladies in the church and mothers of her friends had stepped in.

"They tried to kill us, Cleary." Cavanagh's voice was shaking. "I heard Dad and Grand talking. They tried to burn us alive."

"I know, sweetheart. I know. I thought that James or Will had spoken to you about that."

"They might have. I just wasn't listening to what they said." Cavanagh stared at the soft sage walls with a frown on her face. "We need to find these people. That means we have to put ourselves out there."

"I know, sweetheart. We do have to do that more than we have." Cleary gave a half-hearted grin. "We're dating, Cavanagh. That means our dates will be dangerous. And I don't what that for you."

"I don't want that either. We have the plans that we were given." She looked around at the door. "I think Dad was likely fixing something to eat. Let's go find out if he was and then make some plans. Dad and Grand will not accept that they can't be part of this."

"We can do that." Cleary reached to drop a kiss on her cheek before he pulled her to her feet. He didn't see the surprised look on her face before Cavanagh reached to touch that cheek. "We'll come up with a plan that keeps us as safe as we can be. And I know that Jeff will want to be part of it."

"I worry for him, Cleary." She took back her hand to help her grandfather as he was setting out the plates with a quick and easy meal on them.

"I do too, Cavanagh." Cleary searched the faces of the men in the room with them, realizing that Will and James had joined them. "Will? James? I didn't know that you were here. I'm not sure that I like this."

"No, I don't think that you will. We need to make some plans, Cleary, Cavanagh. Those plans need to be made tonight." Will was exhausted and in pain to some degree. "James has some information that he needs to share with you. And at some point, we will have to accept that someone wants one of us dead. Which one of us that is? It's either you or Cavanagh, Cleary. My thoughts are that it's Cavanagh but it could be you as well."

Will's words dampened the atmosphere in the kitchen as they sat down at the table. The meal was picked at, no one wanting to eat. Foley and Dagen cleared away the remnants of the meal and then sat back down at the table before their hearts were bowed as they sought protection and answers. They just didn't think that they would have that at this point.

Cavanagh raised her head at last, her eyes on Will and then James. She was troubled, to say the least, not sure what to think or say. She had come to that conclusion, that someone wanted her dead. She just couldn't put a finger on who or why.

"James?" Dagen's voice broke through the silence. "What can you tell us?"

James looked around the circle, taking in the emotions that each one was trying hard to hide. They weren't doing very well at that. He sighed. He had not wanted to be here but he had been told that he needed to speak to the trio that night. It was getting too dangerous for them to be out and about. But everyone acknowledged that was exactly what they would do. Will would be back on his investigations. Cavanagh would be back out there changing locks. And Cleary would be back out there with his surveying. There just wasn't enough information to tuck the three of them away somewhere.

Chapter 34

The next evening, Cleary and Cavanagh walked boldly through the downtown area. Their hands were linked. Will walked beside them, his eyes alert to anyone who might mean the three of them harm. Cleary and Will had shared a look over the top of Cavanagh's head, both determined to protect the lady between them. Cleary had had a long talk with Cavanagh at lunch that day, pouring out his heart to her. Cavanagh had wept before she just reached to hug him. Her own words tumbled out as she poured out her heart to him.

Cleary fingered the box in his pocket. He had paid a visit to the bank after lunch and pulled the box from his safety deposit box. He had taken the box out to keep all his valuable items in. That included the jewelry that his mother had passed on to him before she had died. His foster mother had kept it for him over the years.

Will's thoughts drifted to what had been going on and how he had become involved. He shouldn't have been but he was. And he wanted whoever it was that was behind it all. They were inching closer to knowing who it was. They were just not quite there.

Cavanagh was happy. She was loved and loved in return. Cleary was trying hard to protect her. She knew that it was who he was to do that. She wanted this, whatever this was, that they were involved in to be over so that they could go on with their lives. She was on the outlook for whoever it was but wasn't sure that she would recognize that person.

"Cleary? Where are we going?" Cavanagh's voice held a touch of laughter. She didn't know what Cleary had in mind. He had not shared that with her.

"For dinner, at the very least. Will is hungry." Cleary's voice held the laughter that he was trying hard to stifle. He could hear Will's laughter at his words.

Cavanagh's steps slowed as she passed a business that was closed. She stared at the business name and then at the window. Something about that name was familiar to her. She wasn't sure why.

Will stared at Cavanagh and then at the store name. He began to nod. This name was connected to the Lockyers, he knew that from his own investigation. He would need to reach out to James the next day.

Cleary stared at Cavanagh and then Will. Obviously they were making a connection that he wasn't.

"Cavanagh? Will? What is this place?"

"The owners are part of the Lockyer family on their maternal side. I was looking into them before this all broke apart." Will was frustrated and worried. He wasn't on the investigation any more and wanted to be. He wouldn't be allowed to, that much he knew.

Cleary nodded, not wanting to pry into anything that he shouldn't. He felt a tug on his hand and looked at Cavanagh who was trying to move him along the sidewalk, dodging the other pedestrians as she did so.

Sliding onto a chair in a diner, Cavanagh watched the two men with her. Both were agitated, she could tell. She could only pray for God's peace and that He would unlock the doors that were needed to solve this and solve this soon.

Will searched the customers in the diner as the trio placed their order. He listened to the quiet conversation between Cavanagh and Cleary. He frowned as he heard Cleary's question.

"What was that you said, Cleary?" Will waited for Cleary to speak.

"I asked Cavanagh about that store and the owners. I wanted to know about the owner."

Cavanagh nodded. She knew some of the history of the people. Will would likely know the same but perhaps he knew more.

"The store? It's been operating for over fifty years, if I remember correctly." Will's forehead furrowed as he thought through the information that he knew about the family. "They are related to the Lockyer family, but not that close. I think that they are cousins removed at least three or four times."

Cavanagh was nodding. She agreed with that assessment.

"I think that you are correct, Will. I don't remember seeing them around town much in the last couple of years, though. I had heard that they were not involved in the day-to-day operations of the store. Instead they use managers to do that."

"That's what I have heard. I haven't seen them around much either." Will was frustrated at that. He needed to speak with them or rather, James did, and they couldn't track them down. Their whereabouts were well hidden.

"I think that they had property on the other side of the province, near Ottawa. Have you looked for them there?" Cavanagh reached for her fork, ready to start eating. She paused as Cleary prayed over their food.

Will stared at her. He had not been aware of that. His phone was out as he sent off a quick text to James.

"I didn't know that. And I don't know that James knew that." Will began to eat, listening to the quiet conversation around them before his head tilted. His eyes searched for the woman that he could hear speaking. He frowned at the woman, seeing her watching him and then nodding. She had spoken in the way that she had to get his attention. Will knew her and would pass her name onto James who would then speak with her.

Cleary rose at last, not satisfied that they had accomplished anything. Will waved as he walked away, leaving Cavanagh standing as tight to Cleary as she could.

"Cleary? Did we succeed in anything tonight?" Cavanagh stared around, feeling watched but not seeing anyone other than the townspeople whom she knew.

"I don't know, Cavanagh. I really don't know. I pray that we did. I want this over yesterday. You're in danger and I want that over for you and your father and grandfather. I can't do that for you. The investigation seems to have stalled."

"It has." Cavanagh walked quickly forward, heading towards Cleary had parked. Her feet slowed and then she pulled him into the entrance of a store, not taking her eyes from his car.

"Cavanagh?" Cleary was not certain what she was attempting to do. He peeked around the wall, a frown on his face. He was not seeing what Cavanagh was.

"There are men by your car. I know them. They're part of the underground and criminal aspect of town. They're not waiting there for our good." Cavanagh's voice was no louder than a whisper, causing Cleary to lean closer to understand her words. "How do we get to your car and then get away?"

Cleary peeked around the building edge once more, monitoring the situation. He grabbed for Cavanagh's hand as the men disappeared, running towards his car. His key fob clicked as he unlocked the doors, shoving Cavanagh in on the driver's side and then sliding in. The door was slammed shut as he keyed the motor to life and then took off, heading not for Cavanagh's home or his but for her father's. Once he parked, he was around the car and pulling Cavanagh from it and running towards the front door of the house where Foley was standing and waiting for them.

"Cavanagh? Cleary?" Foley wasn't sure what was happening. It just seemed as if the two were in danger.

“Inside, Foley.” Cleary slid to a halt on the wooden hallway floor. “We just made it away from the downtown area. I don’t know that we were followed, but we could have been.” Cleary wrapped Cavanagh into a hug.

“What?” Foley was disturbed. “What are you talking about?”

“Some men were around Cleary’s car. We managed o get away but I’m not sure if they followed us.” Cavanagh crept to the window, turning off the light in the hall and peeking around the curtain. “I don’t see anyone but that doesn’t mean that they’re not out there.”

Chapter 35

Cavanagh moved through the next few days, knowing that she was being followed but not caring. In fact, she deliberately went out of her way to ensure that she had a shadow. She also knew that both Cleary and Will would be upset with her.

Cleary had it figured out and was doing the same. He worried about Jeff and had had a long talk with Jeff and his father. Both of them had indicated that they were aware of the danger but were willing to chance it with Cleary. Will had spoken with them and advised all three that off-duty officers were following both Cleary and Cavanagh. They just would not see them. Cleary had nodded. It was about what he had expected. He just didn't want it.

Foley stood and watched his daughter working away in the shop one day, tidying away the work orders from the day. He worried about her but knew that he could not stop her from being out in the community, doing what she did best.

"Cavanagh? What is your feeling right now?" Foley waited patiently for his daughter to speak. Dagen was not in the shop that day, electing to take the day off.

"My feeling? I'm not sure what you mean, Dad." Cavanagh turned to her father, seeing the worry that he was trying so hard to hide.

"Your feeling about all this. I know you well enough to know that you do have feelings about this."

"I do, Dad." Cavanagh squinted at the clock. "It's close enough to quitting. Let's lock up and head for my place. I have some information that I would like to run past you."

"Sounds like a plan."

The two moved around, turning on the security system and then heading out. Cavanagh paused beside her car for a moment, her thoughts tumbling over and over. She wasn't clear on what she thought or knew. That was where her father came in. She had always done that, discussed her feelings, thoughts, and worries with him.

Cleary rose from where he had seated himself on her front steps and hugged her. He shared a look with Foley before nodding. They were meeting that night to discuss what they were going through. It affected not just the younger couple. It affected her father and grandfather as well. They had had some discussions but not in depth. Cleary had information that a friend had sent on to him and he was grateful for that. It would help, he knew, to make their discussion more in depth and possibly help them to reach a conclusion on what they needed to do to end this.

Cavanagh worked away on a meal, just some beef stew and fresh bread that she had prepared the night before. She wasn't hungry and doubted that the two men were hungry. But they would all eat in an effort to keep everything as normal as they could.

Their meal over, the three bowed their heads. They needed to feel the presence of God in a way that they had never before. They looked up at one another before Cavanagh rose and headed for her office, returning with a pile of papers that she dropped on the tabletop. Cleary had retrieved his briefcase.

Foley reached for the papers and sorted through them. He added the ones that Cleary had pulled out of the briefcase. He handed out the copies to each of them and then began to read. Foley began to make notes, nodding as he read through the conclusions that the two had come to.

Cleary studied the information that his friend had sent him. It puzzled him. She had named other people in the town who she suspected were involved. She had passed that information on to the investigative team in his town. It was what he had expected her to do.

Foley's finger paused at a name. He frowned, struggling to remember the relationship between that person and the Lockyer house. He nodded at last. He had the connection.

"Cavanagh, this name? The Stuart named here? He's a cousin to the Lockyer who owns the house. He's been upstanding in the community. It may be that he is hiding his activities. We'll need James to research that."

Cleary turned to that page, a frown on his face. He didn't know the name but obviously Cavanagh and Foley did.

"What can you tell me about this man?" Cleary looked at Cavanagh, seeing the struggle that she was going through. "Cavanagh?"

"I went through school with his family. A son and a daughter. The daughter hated me and I never knew why. The son didn't have anything to do with me." Her head went down on her folded arms. A deep sigh shook her body.

"I never knew that, Cavanagh." Foley reached to rub his daughter's back, a motion that had calmed her as a child.

Cavanagh raised her head, staring at Cleary. He didn't know the town or the people. She reached for her phone and sent off a quick text message to both Will and James. Will would remember that family. He had had interactions with the daughter. Cavanagh shared a look with her father.

"Dad? What do you know about them?"

Foley shrugged. He had had little contact with the family. Over the years, there had been interactions when they needed locksmith work. Those contacts had been few and far between. His eyes dropped back to the paperwork and he continued to read through it. Foley sat back when he finished, studying the younger couple in front of him. He gave a small smile. Cleary had reached for Cavanagh's hand at some point and her fingers were curled around his.

Cavanagh frowned at what she was reading. She went back to the beginning of the section that she had been reading and reread it. She continued to frown.

"Dad? Who are the Phillips?"

"The Phillips? They were one of the founders of the local paper mill. I know it's not working now other than as a landmark and tourist attraction. At one time, it employed a number of workers. They did take care of their workers. When the mill closed, it was hard for some of the older workers to cope. The Phillips took care of those workers." Foley thought back over the years. "That was about twenty-five years ago. I don't know that you remember."

"I think that I do. That girl? Her father was one of the workers who lost his job. She seemed to resent the fact that you had a thriving business. I don't know why she had that attitude. It wasn't your fault." Cavanagh felt Cleary's hand tighten on hers in an effort to bring comfort to her.

"I never knew that happened, Cavanagh. You never said." Foley was distraught at that. He began to pray for healing for his daughter. There were just so many areas that she needed that, it appeared.

"It's okay, Dad. I never let her get to me. But how does this all fit into what we're going through? We need to narrow it down in names but how do we do that?"

Chapter 36

Cavanagh studied the thick wooden door that she was standing in front of, working to change the lockset to something more decorative. She usually enjoyed this part of her work. Today, she wasn't. She felt someone watching her and that caused her distress. Cavanagh knew that she was at risk out there and that if someone went after her, an innocent bystander could be harmed. She turned as she heard footsteps and frowned at the off-duty officer who stood there.

"Jake? What are you doing here?"

Jake grinned at her. He was a close friend of hers and had volunteered to provide security for her that day. He had tracked down Foley who had sent him Cavanagh's way.

"I'm your security today, Cavanagh. Will and James asked for volunteers. I've always wanted to see how you work your magic with the locks." He continued to grin at her as she snorted.

"Like you had to do this? You could have done a ride-along at any time." Cavanagh turned to face the street and shuddered. Jake's eyes narrowed as he saw the shudder. "Someone is following me today, Jake. I don't know who or why."

Jake nodded. This was why he had felt compelled to track his friend down. He knew that Will was off duty that day and had headed for Cleary.

"I see. Let me walk around the area while you're working here. Do you have much longer?" Jake waited patiently for Cavanagh to process his words. She was like that at times, he knew, thinking through what she had been asked before she responded.

"I have this one just about done and then I need to move to the back door. That one shouldn't take too long. Then I'm off for a store down town." She frowned again. "Jake, when did Mrs. Peters sell her shop?"

"Her shop? I didn't know that she had. I saw her heading in there as I drove past." Jake froze in place before his phone was out. This smelled like a set up and he was afraid for the elderly lady who ran the used book shop. "James? Mrs. Peters may be in danger. Cavanagh is supposed to head there to change locks. Mrs. Peters hasn't retired."

James was on his feet, knowing that this just might be the turning point that they were waiting for. He pointed at two officers who were just finishing up paperwork.

"You two, you're with me. Head for Mrs. Peters' shop. She may well be in danger." Will ran for his car, dreading the uppermost thought in his mind.

Will shoved open the book store door and entered, the two officers behind them. They began a systematic search before Will heard his name called and ran towards the back office. He slid to a stop, staring down at the huddled form that was Mrs. Peters.

"Is she alive?" Will could barely get out the words. Mrs. Peters had been a big part of his life and that of the community.

"She is. She's been knocked out." The officer twisted on his heel to stare up at Will. "Who did this?"

"Someone after Cavanagh. Jake called me. Cavanagh had a work order to change the locks here. She was puzzled because she hadn't heard that Mrs. Peters had sold the shop." Will walked away, his phone turning over in his hand before he was calling Jake. "Jake? It was a set up. Mrs. Peters is hurt. I suspect that Cavanagh would have disappeared again if she had shown up here."

Jake's face tightened at that. They were all aware of what was going on with Cavanagh and wanted it over for her. It just didn't seem to end.

"Let me know how she is. I'll stay with Cavanagh. She feels as if she is being watched and I am certain that she is." Jake turned to watch Cavanagh as she packed away her tools before she reached to pick up her kits and head around the house. "She's almost done at this place. Lynda dropped me off so I'll ride with her." Lynda was Jake's wife and also a good friend to Cavanagh.

"Do that. Will is with Cleary, although I'm not sure that is such a good idea." James walked back through the shop, intent on the paramedics as they worked on Mrs. Peters who was now alert and insisting that she didn't need to go to the hospital. She was over-ruled and James reached for her keys to lock up the store.

James stood on the sidewalk before he walked down the alley to the back of the building. A thought had crossed his mind. He studied the buildings and then nodded. Someone had been waiting there, he knew, and had disappeared when the emergency vehicles had shown up. When would it end for his friends? All he could do was trust God and rely on His promises. He knew from his conversations with both Cleary and Cavanagh that they were delving deeper into those promises. Their peace in this situation was evident. They had learned to trust God in a deeper and wider way. James needed to do some delving as well, he decided.

Cavanagh looked around at Jake before her concentration went back to her work. She was heading back to the shop after this, she decided. She would take her father's offer to go out to the work sites. She felt too dangerous to be out and about and around people.

"Cavanagh?" Jake paused beside her as she was once more packing up her tools. "James called."

"And what did he have to say this time?" Cavanagh was frustrated. Her words had a bite to them that they normally didn't have.

"Mrs. Peters was assaulted this morning and knocked out. She is on her feet and being assessed. We need to get you back to your shop." Jake's voice and face were stern. He was expecting a fight from Cavanagh before she would agree.

"I know, Jake. I'm not safe out here. And no one around me is. I'm heading for the shop. Dad said that he'd take over the out-of-shop work. He'll feel better if I'm somewhere I can lock myself away." Cavanagh blinked against the sudden tears that clouded her vision. "I don't get it, Jake. Why is God allowing this?"

"We don't know, Cavanagh. We may not fully understand His reasons. We can trust and walk forward hand in hand with HIm. We also have the confidence that He never leaves us alone in anything that we face." Jake watched her face, seeing the struggle that she was in the middle of.

Cavanagh nodded. Jake had expressed what she was learning over and over again. She wanted to be free to live her life. She didn't feel that way.

"I know, Jake. It's hard when you're going through this. I have connected with a group of ladies who are helping me. One of the from Elmton has threatened to send in her husband's security team."

"That might not be a bad idea." Jake grinned at the glare sent his way.

"I know that. I don't understand. I am trying to keep in mind that God is in control and that He allows the rain to fall on the good and bad. I worry about Cleary and about Dad and Grand. They could be hurt because of me. And we don't have an answer as to why it's happening." Cavanagh reached to pick up her kits and headed for the van. She shoved them inside and then closed and locked the door. Her gaze went around the area. Someone was out there and too close for her to feel comfortable. Her keys were taken from her hand before Jake shoved her into the passenger seat and then ran around to climb in and drive away.

Chapter 37

Cleary walked back towards his truck, his steps slow and weighted. It had been a bad day all around. The neighbour to the property that he had been surveying had been brash and in his face as soon as he arrived. Cleary had struggled to remain calm as the man unleashed venom on him. Jeff had stared at the man and then at Cleary before he moved to help. This had delayed their work on that property. Will had appeared at some point just as the man shoved Cleary and landed his boot in Cleary's side as he fell, his balance off when the shove was initiated. Cleary had sat up and watched in disbelief as the man had struggled with Will and then the responding officers, his vile curses darkening the air around him.

"Sorry about that, Jeff. You shouldn't have been exposed to that." Cleary struggled for words. His ribs were bruised and hurting.

"It's called life, Cleary. I can't be kept hidden from this." Jeff was understanding of Cleary's words. "I don't know what his problem was but he's been a troublemaker for years. This time? He'll go away for a while. Assaulting you and then Will and the other officers? That's the final straw for him."

"He will? That's interesting. I was beginning to think that I had done something." Cleary concentrated on his paperwork for a moment before he raised his head. "Jeff? When do you go to college?"

"Next fall. I am doing my other course work on line. The school approved that. Do you need me to keep working for you?" Jeff held his breath, praying that Cleary would say yes.

"I do. Even when you're in college, I would like to have you around when you can. You can take the course here?"

"I can. We have a really good college in town." Jeff bit at his lip. "Do you have any sense that they are close to finding whoever it is?"

Cleary shook his head. He too was frustrated at that and wanted to meet with James. Only James didn't seem ready to meet with him. He would find Cavanagh, he decided, and go from there. He glanced at Jeff, a thought running through his mind.

"Jeff, you and your friends are out and about in the town. I think that we have been remiss in not talking with you. How be you round up as many of them as you can, guy and gal, and meet at my place? I'll barbecue for a meal and then we'll talk."

Jeff grinned at Cleary. That was what he had been wanting to do. He just hadn't felt comfortable enough to ask Cleary if they could.

"We're ready to meet with you, Cleary. We've been working on our own on this. And Cavanagh and her father and grandfather need to be there."

Cleary grinned at the enthusiasm that Jeff was showing. The youth were out and about in the town, hearing information and conversations. People tended to ignore the youth as not being a source of information. Cleary had always thought differently than that. A quick text to Cavanagh confirmed that they would be there. He hesitated for a moment before he looked over at Jeff.

"Do we need Will or Jamcs?"

"Not yet. Let's look at what we have and then we can pass that on. One of my friends has been working on a database of names. She'll bring that as well." Jeff was willing to do what he could to help Cleary. His friends had become part of Cleary's friend circle because of Jeff and they too wanted to help.

Cavanagh looked around at the group that had gathered at Cleary's that night. She gave a brief smile. She knew the teens, having been involved in their group at church. They were good kids, she knew, but she worried about them getting involved in something like this. The risk of harm to them was great.

The teens' laughter spilled through the house as they teased one another and then the adults. Cleary's grin was out in force, even though he grimaced at times at the pain from where he was kicked. He caught Cavanagh watching him and knew that he would need to confess to her what had happened. Dagen and Foley just stepped in as grandfathers to the teens. They too had known the teens since they had been born and were welcomed as friends by said teens.

Cavanagh approached Jeff, a smile on her face as he grinned at her.

"Jeff? What have you been up to?"

Jeff shrugged, his eyes on his best friend, Jason.

"We've been working this for you and Cleary, Cavanagh. People talk around us. They don't think that kids matter or that they will say anything. We want to help. Susie has been working on a database with names and what we knew." Jeff pointed at Susie who sat at the kitchen table, a laptop open in front of her. "She wants to go over this with you."

Cavanagh was in a chair beside Susie almost before Jeff finished speaking. Susie grinned at her as she turned her laptop more towards Cavanagh.

"This is what we have come up with. Jeff was a great source of information from what he learned from Cleary and you. Take a look at it." Susie was apprehensive for a moment before Cavanagh reached to hug the teen.

"Okay, let's see what you have. You're brilliant at this, did you know that?" Cavanagh didn't see the surprised and then the pleased looks that crossed Susie's face. "You have organized better than an adult would. Can we print it?"

"We can. I just need to connect to Cleary's wifi if he lets me." Susie looked up as a piece of paper was waved in her face. Cleary grinned at her surprise. "Thanks, Cleary. How many copies?"

"One for each of us, please, Susie. Don't worry about the paper or ink. I have plenty." Cleary walked away, Foley following him to help collate the papers. Cleary didn't speak for a moment.

"Jeff told me what happened today, Cleary. I'm sorry that it did. That man has always had a mean temper and is an alcoholic to boot. He's a mean drunk as they say and anyone who gets in his way pays the price."

"I'm glad it was me and not Jeff. Jeff didn't need to see that." Cleary was still troubled by the incident.

"Don't worry about Jeff. He's seen a lot worse. His father's brother drank away his life. He did what happened today many times and much worse. He died about four years ago. Unfortunately, he never did reform himself despite being raised the same as Jeff's father. Their parents were great Christians, active in the church, but their two sons came first."

Cleary nodded. Jeff had talked with him that day about his uncle. He had been afraid of him, he had admitted, when he was younger and hated his uncle for the disruption he always caused in the family. Cleary had simply asked if Jeff had asked for forgiveness for his hatred. Jeff had nodded. He had battled it out with God and had come through victorious in that.

Chapter 38

Cavanagh paced her home office during the night. She had retired but had only had broken sleep. She finally rose and dressed, heading for the kitchen to make herself coffee. The largest cup that she could find was in her hand as she paced. Her thoughts were troubled. Pausing at her desk, she stared down at the papers that came from Susie's database. That young lady had worked hard with the other teens to correlate and confirm what information that they could. Cavanagh had no idea how they had managed to do that but they had.

Her index finger flipped through the paperwork. The answer was there, Cavanagh was convinced. She sat, her cup landing on the desk before she pulled the stack of papers towards her. She gave a smile as she thought of the teens the evening before. She loved them all but this had made them even more special to her.

Cavanagh began to read through the names and what information was there. She paused as a name, her face paling as she did so. This person? They were related to both families. She just had to prove it. A chime from her computer caught her attention and she pulled up her email program. A frown covered her face.

Emma had explained about her business of finding people and places when they had first met. She provided confirmation of the name that Cavanagh had focused on. Emma had also stated that the information she was giving Cavanagh had also gone on to the local investigator. Would it help, she asked, to solve the mystery?

Cavanagh's fingers flew across the keyboard as she responded, thanking Emma for passing on that information. She printed it off and then added it to the stack. She reached for it but instead, her head went down on her folded arms as she sobbed. The stress and worry and fear had gotten the best of her as she brought everything to her Heavenly Father. After a time, her sobs quietened and she waited for the peace of God that she needed. Two hours later, Cavanagh's head was raised. Determination sat on it as she found her phone and sent off a text to her father that she would not be in that day and that she planned to spend that day in studying what she had.

Foley stared at the text message that morning before he nodded. This was his Cavanagh, he decided, fighting to find the answers of what this all meant. He sighed as well. This wasn't over for the couple and he was deeply afraid for them.

Cleary walked towards his home at the end of the day. It had been a much better day, he decided. Jeff and he had talked over what the teens had found. Cleary found Jeff giving answers in a clear and concise manner, something that he would have expected from someone twenty years Jeff's senior. He nodded at his thoughts. He needed to find Cavanagh though and see what she had to say.

Cavanagh looked up as Cleary stopped in front of her. She had asked Will to drop her off at Cleary's when he had stopped by that afternoon. She had shaken her head at his questions, not willing to speak with him. Will had let her away with that, simply stating that they would talk and that talk would happen in the next two days.

Cleary's face lit up before he hugged his lady and dropped a kiss on her cheek.

"You're here, Cavanagh. I was going to come and find you." He looked around, frowning as he didn't see her car.

"Will dropped me off. We need to talk, Cleary." Cavanagh's hands held the paperwork that she had spent the day working through. She had a good idea now who was behind it all. She didn't have the reason.

"And we will. Let me get cleaned up and then I'm taking you out for a meal. We'll talk, sweetheart. I promise you that." Cleary was away and back in short order, locking his front door behind him. He sat beside Cavanagh for a moment. "What did you discover?" His voice was soft as he asked that question, his arm coming around her.

"I know who it is. I just don't know why." Cavanagh leaned against Cleary, drawing from his strength for a moment. "I need to let James know. I just don't know how to."

"Talk to me and then we'll face him together. I'm not working tomorrow. I needed to do some office work. Jeff had to be away anyway. Talk to me tonight. We'll pray it through together and then tomorrow, we'll find James." He dropped another kiss on her cheek.

"Thank you, Cleary, for being who you are." Cavanagh didn't want to stand up and move away from Cleary but she had to.

Cleary was on his feet, a hand reaching for Cavanagh's. He tucked her inside his truck and then moved to sit behind the steering wheel. He was troubled, he knew, about what their conversation would be like. He didn't want any more worry or harm to come to his lady. He didn't think that could be avoided, however.

The next day, Will stood at Cleary's door, his finger hitting the door bell once more. He had already punched at it a number of times. Cleary's truck was in the garage as he had already determined. He didn't see Cavanagh's car. She had stated that she was heading for Cleary's place when they had spoken just after nine.

Will turned and stepped away from the house, walking around it. He didn't see anything concerning but that didn't mean something had not happened. He tried the knob to the back door, surprised to find it turning under his hand. He stepped inside, not hearing any noise. Will called for both Cleary and Cavanagh as he walked through the tastily-decorated house. He paused in the kitchen. Cleary and Cavanagh were not there. And neither one was answering their phones. They went straight to voice mail.

Walking from the house, Will began a systematic search around it and the rest of the yard. He hesitated for a moment as he stood at the garage, facing the door that lead into it. He felt sudden fear for his friends and began to pray for them.

Finally, his hand reached for the door, shoving it open. He stepped into the dimness, not hearing anything. His hand reached for the light switch. The overhead light flicked on, shining into the dark corners. Will walked forward, searching for what he was not sure of. He stared down at the debris beside Cleary's truck before he stepped back and then walked from the garage.

The garage was now a crime scene. It was obvious that something had happened and that something had happened to Cleary and Cavanagh. Will made the call that he had to but he also began to pray harder for the two. He was well aware that they were learning to trust God in a deeper way. It was no consolation at the moment with the two missing once more.

Chapter 39

Foley stared at Will in shock. His mouth opened and closed as he fought his emotions, unable to speak. Dagen stood beside him, shock on his face as well.

"What are you saying, Will?" Dagen spoke for his son.

"Cleary and Cavanagh have disappeared. I was to meet them about an hour ago. They weren't there. I found evidence that they were once more abducted. The team is working there now." Will's face show how disturbed he was.

"What can we do?" Foley found his voice at last. He was more than a little worried about his daughter. This should not have happened again. She had been through enough without this.

"I talked to the pastor. He's setting up a room at the church for day and night prayer sessions. You are welcome to join them there. Other than that, we need to keep you two safe. If Cavanagh does not cooperate with whatever they want her to do, you and Dagen may well become targets. And we don't want anything to happen to you. James will reach out to you in the next hour or so." Will walked away, not satisfied with what he had been able to tell them.

Foley and Dagen stared at one another. They had no idea what to do or where to turn. Foley reached to lock the door to the shop. He headed for his vehicle as did Dagen. They were not sure where to go or what to do.

Dagen stopped his son with a hand to his arm.

"Wait, Foley. Where are we going?"

Foley stopped, his head dropping forward. He studied the pavement under his feet. He had no idea where to go or what to do. He wanted Cavanagh back home. Foley just didn't know where to go to find her.

"I don't know, Dad. At this point, I don't know." Foley reached to wipe the tears from his face.

Dagen reached for his son, wrapping him into a hug. Foley clung to his father as sobs shook his body. He didn't know how to comfort his son other than beg God for that peace and comfort that only He could provide. He had to pray that way. There was no other way to pray.

Will approached James as he stood outside Cleary's garage. The large door had been raised as the team worked away.

"James?"

"Will?" James turned his head slightly. "Dagen and Foley?"

"I sent them to the church. I'm not sure that they will head that way. Now, what do we have here?" Will nodded towards the garage.

"I am really not sure what we have. There is the evidence beside his truck. It almost seems as if they were trying to escape and didn't make it." James was frustrated. This was not to have happened.

"I know. I wish it hadn't. Cavanagh told me that she had arrived at a name and wanted to meet with me today. We were meeting here." Will spun in a circle. "We're being monitored."

"We are. I wonder if they're on our side or against us." James gave a quick grin at Will's snort. "I think that we are being watched by someone trying to help us."

"I think that you are right." Will paused for a moment. "What if it wasn't someone who wanted to harm them who took them? What if it was someone who was trying to protect them? And they took them from here."

James stared at Will in disbelief. That didn't happen, did it? But as he continued to digest that, he began to nod. It was possible that could be the case. The question was who? James looked at Will as he said a name, shocked at who he had named.

Pulling Will with him, he pointed at their vehicles and was speeding off shortly, Will on his tail. Once in his office, James reached to type in the name into one of the programs that he used. He read through the information that he found, Will standing at his shoulder and reading as well.

Will began to nod. This person? They needed to find her. But she was a difficult person to find or contact. She was a recluse, not out in the community much at all.

"She'll be difficult to approach. I used to mow her lawn when I was a teen." Will's thoughts went back to the past. "I can approach her, I think."

"Try that, Will. See if she knows anything at all. We may be on the wrong track though." James sat back in his chair.

"We might be. But I do need to try this." Will walked away, heading for his office. He spent time in prayer, begging God to help him do what was right in this and that God would lead to where the couple were.

On his feet, Will headed for a house on the edge of town. He walked up to the door and rang the old-fashioned door bell without any response. He waited and then left, no one answering his repeated knocks.

Will sat in his car, studying the house and then the surrounding property. The woman who lived there was home, Will was certain about that. She wouldn't answer the door, that was also obvious. How did he reach out to her and get her to open up to him? Will knew that she remembered him. He had stopped by a few months ago, just to reassure himself that she was fine. He could see the early signs of ill health but because he was not a family member, he couldn't do much. He had reached out to a niece but didn't know if anything had been followed up on.

James turned from his computer, shaking his head. He had traced the lady back to the Locker family. He wondered if Will was aware of it. He reached for his phone, intent on reaching out to Will only to find that man walking into his office and sitting down.

"Will?" James questioned him with only his name spoken.

“I couldn’t get an answer. I was sure that she was there. The house seems lived in.” Will looked up and frowned at James.

“I guess that she was but didn’t want to talk to you. I found out something interesting.” James handed over the information that he had printed without saying anything. He watched Will intently, seeing the instance that he caught the implications.

“She’s related to the Lockyers? How did we not know this?” Will was troubled deeply by this.

“We had no way of knowing this, Will.” James sighed. “We need to talk with her. I don’t know how we are going to manage that.”

Chapter 40

The day that they disappeared once more, Cleary had headed to pick up Cavanagh and had taken her out for breakfast and then headed for his home. He pulled into the garage and turned to her, his mouth opened to speak. He snapped it closed as he stared at the man standing at Cavanagh's open door. She looked at him with fear on her face.

Cleary's hands went up as he heard the door behind him open. He was ordered out of his truck and obeyed, his hands still in the air. Cavanagh was shoved around the truck to stand behind him, her hands raised as well.

Forced into a truck, Cleary reached for Cavanagh's hand, his eyes alert to where they were being taken. He could hear Cavanagh's indrawn breath as they were pulled from the truck and shoved toward a house. He frowned at it, recognizing it as one of the old show places in town.

Cavanagh roamed the room that they were shoved into, trying to find a way out. Only there didn't seem to be one. Cleary stopped her at last, a hand on her arm.

"Is this really that house?" Cleary was in disbelief at the thought of who owned the house and wondered how she was involved.

"It is. And she's related to the Lockyers. I don't know that she's involved. She's been a recluse for years." Cavanagh turned into his hug, hugging him tightly. “She won’t come near us but I wonder how she is involved.” She stared up at Cleary. “Cleary, I know that God is here with us. I know that He will unlock the doors to the mystery soon. I just wish it was now. I am so afraid of what will happen. How do we escape this?”

“We don’t. God frees us at His will. He protects us whatever we are going through. He gives His peace to us. We can be surrounded by danger and storms but He calms us in the midst of them as well as calming the storms.” Cleary’s hug tightened on her. “We have to trust Him as hard as it is sometimes.”

“I know, Cleary. I know. It’s hard though.” Cavanagh moved from the safety of Cleary’s arms, searching for a way out. “We need to get away, Cleary. How?”

Cleary nodded. He too walked the room, searching for an exit. He paused at a window, his hand on the strip of wood that held the windows in place. He felt Cavanagh’s hand on his back before he was digging out his pocket knife. His father had been a carpenter and Cleary knew that if he could remove the strips of wood, then he had a good chance of removing the window. They were old wooden windows that Cleary’s father had dealt with many times with his son’s assistance.

Cavanagh watched with interest how Cleary managed to remove the strips of wood with his pocket knife. She hovered between the door to the room and being at Cleary’s side. Cleary set the strips of wood to one side and then worked to ease the window from the frame. He set it to one side before he leaned out and looked around. He felt it was safe for them to drop down to the ground that wasn't really that far down.

Cleary dropped through the window and reached back to catch Cavanagh as she dropped down. He reached for her hand and ran for the house next door to them and then kept running down the street.

Cavanagh pulled Cleary to a halt at last and around to the back of a large oak tree. She leaned against it, struggling to regain her breath. Her eyes were huge as she stared at Cleary.

"Did we really just do that?"

Cleary hugged her tightly. He was struggling to breathe as well. They had run from the house and kept running until they felt that they were safe.

"We did. Why were we taken there?" Cleary was puzzled at that. He didn't know the history of the house.

"She's related to the Lockyers. Not close, I don't think. She's a recluse, rarely leaving her home. I don't know if she's one of the bad guys or not." She stared at him. "How did you know what to do with the windows?"

"The windows?" Cleary began to grin. "Dad was a carpenter and did renovations on a lot of old houses. I was with him working alongside of him when I could. He taught me that." Cleary thanked God for his father and his training.

"Thank God that you were. Now, we're getting close to the downtown area. Should we find Will or James?"

Cleary shrugged. He reached for her hand and headed down the sidewalk. He drew in a deep breath of the crisp air. He wanted this over. Cleary wanted to go on walks just like with Cavanagh. He wanted to date her and then if God was willing, to marry her.

Cavanagh pulled him to a stop near the police department building. She bit at her lip, a sign that she was troubled by a decision that she was trying to make. She shared a look with Cleary who simply shrugged and then pulled her towards the building.

Will stopped in his walk back to his office, his eyes on the couple ahead of him. He gave a shout and then ran towards them. He slid to a halt, shock on his face as they turned to him.

"Cleary? Cavanagh? Where do you two come from?" Will could barely get out his words.

"We escaped, Will. It was just so strange. Can we get inside? Someone is watching us." Cavanagh looked around as she spoke, her free hand rubbing at her arm.

"We can. In we go." Will rushed them inside, reaching for visitors badges for them. Then, he almost shoved them down the hall to James' office.

James looked up in surprise before he was on his feet. Shock coloured his face for a moment before he frowned.

"What are you two doing here?" He watched as the couple shared a look.

"We were taken from Cleary's garage. I think that we left a mess on the floor." Cavanagh looked distressed at that. “Then, we were taken to the other Lockyer place. The one where Mrs. Eden has lived for years. I know that she is related to them. I just don’t know if she’s on their side or not.”

“I would say no, Cavanagh.” Cleary spoke up, his eyes on the two detectives. “I don’t think that we were taken to harm us. It felt more as if we were taken to keep us safe. The three men didn’t show us any weapons. We just went along with them without really being threatened.”

Cavanagh nodded. That was what she had thought. She didn’t know how they would prove it. She turned to Will.

“You used to do her lawn, Will. Would she have done this?”

Will nodded. There had been rumours over the years about a vendetta that she had against portions of her family but those rumours had never been proven. They had been put down to her eccentricity.

Chapter 41

James regained his chair after handing the couple icy cold bottles of water. He leaned forward, eager to hear what had happened. He frowned as he listened to what they had to say. A hand went up at one point.

"Cleary. Explain again about the windows. I'm not seeing what you're saying."

Cleary nodded. It was hard to follow his words, he knew. On his feet, he was at the window to James' office.

"It's like this. With the old-style windows, you don't have the metal frame that we do today. The windows are set into the frame. Thin strips of wood called stops are then placed along the window. This keeps the window in place but allows the window to be raised and lowered. The stops are nailed in. It didn't take much to remove the stops and then the windows. I did it a lot with my Dad. He was a carpenter and taught me a lot, even if just by watching him work."

Cleary reclaimed his seat, his hand reclaiming Cavanagh's. He frowned as he watched Cavanagh retrieve her phone, a surprised look on her face as she answered it and then put it on speaker.

The four in the room listened to the frail, wavering voice that came across the air waves.

"Cavanagh, dear, it's Mrs. Eden. You escaped from the room." They could hear the pleasure in that.

“We did, Mrs. Eden. Who did this? I know it wasn’t you.” Cavanagh’s voice was gentle as she spoke to the elderly lady.

“No, it wasn’t me. I was glad that you were in my house. I thought you would find a way to escape. I can’t talk for long. Roger will be back soon. He’s the one who did it. You need to find him and have him arrested. He’ll keep doing this until you or your young man is dead.” The phone clicked off as she hung up her receiver.

Cavanagh carefully pushed her phone back into her pocket. Mrs. Eden had always been kind to her, even to the present. Cavanagh was one of the few people who were allowed into her home. Cavanagh hated that the memories were tarnished by their recent confinement. She needed to find a way to get Mrs. Eden out of there. Her phone was back out as she called the elderly back.

“Mrs. Eden. You need to leave. I’m coming to get you. Roger won’t be home for an hour. He’ll be out celebrating our captivity. Be ready to leave in fifteen minutes.” Cavanagh turned to Will, who was nodding. He was in agreement with Cavanagh. Mrs. Eden needed to get out of the house and if she went with Cavanagh, that was acceptable.

Heading for Will’s car, the four headed back for Mrs. Eden. That lady was waiting for them, standing on the sidewalk. She slid into the back seat of the car as Cleary slipped out of it and let her in. Cavanagh reached an arm around the lady, almost laughing at the look on Mrs. Eden’s face.

"Now, dear, how do we catch Roger? He's taken over too much of my life as well as yours and your young man. Will? What do you suggest?"

Will was grinning back at Mrs. Eden. This was the lady who he remembered from years past.

"Mrs. Eden, tell me one thing. Was Roger making you stay there?"

Mrs. Eden was nodding.

"He was trying to take over my financial affairs and take all of my money. He resented the fact that he had to work for a living. He has always hated Cavanagh and tried to use this to get back at her. I'm not sure why he would feel like that. He hated you too, Will." Mrs. Eden's eyes had brightened as they drove away from her home. "He kept me a prisoner, Will, and tried to isolate me from everything."

"That's what I wondered." Will turned back to stare out of the front window of the car. His mind was racing as he thought through what they needed to do.

James pulled to a stop at Cavanagh's home and watched as the three in the back seat ran for her home, Cleary helping Mrs. Eden move as quickly as she could. He nodded at Will who was lost in thought.

"Will? We need to find this Roger and then track up the chain of command to the top. And we need to do it now."

Will shook off his thoughts and then spoke.

"Look for him in a bar. He likes his alcohol and always has. Then we look for his uncle and then his great uncle. They are all involved in crime in town.

The uncle has been in and out of jail for as long as I can remember. Let's head in and get what we need." Will watched the traffic pass by before he frowned. "This is not making sense, James. I wonder why Mrs. Eden was involved."

"I think she was involved in helping to protect Cleary and Cavanagh. This last abduction doesn't fit the others." James walked towards his office, Will at his side. "She's not the culprit here. Her family is."

"Roger isn't her family. He's not related to her closely."

James' hand went out as he stopped walking and stopped Will in his tracks.

"He's not a relative? Then how did it get to this point?" James was puzzled by that.

"His mother used to clean for Mrs. Eden. He is very familiar with Mrs. Eden and the house. I heard that he had been living there and couldn't figure it out. I'll work on warrants for that place and the others." Will walked away, desperate to end this adventure before someone was killed.

James nodded before he headed to find his supervisor and then the patrol officer' supervisor. They had an intense meeting, their plans finalized. Will appeared with the warrants, setting off the first of the plans.

Cavanagh hugged Mrs. Eden as that lady stood for a moment in Cavanagh's living room. She was worried about the lady but didn't know what to do about it. Her eyes met those of Cleary who was puzzled by what had transpired that day.

Chapter 42

Cavanagh could not sleep that night. She curled up on the couch, wrapped in a blanket. She could hear soft movement around her in the dim lighting before she felt a hand rest on her head. Foley sat near his daughter, fatigue weighing down his movements, but he would not be anywhere else. Dagen slept in a chair nearby. Cavanagh knew that Cleary was around somewhere, in the office, she decided. He had asked to use her computer to do some research. The couple would need to be at work the next day. She didn't think that any of them would be alert.

Early morning found Will and James tapping at Cavanagh's front door. The two detectives were exhausted but they were also ready to end the adventure that day. They had their plans ready to set in play with the required warrants and teams waiting for the go ahead to move in.

Cavanagh cracked open her door and then stepped to one side to let the detectives in. She saw the patrol vehicles parked in her driveway and on the street. She drew in a deep breath before turning to Will.

"Will?" Cavanagh felt Cleary's arms come around her.

"We're moving in this morning, Cavanagh. We need all of you to stay here unless there is an emergency. Contact whoever it is that you need to and cancel any appointments that you have for the day. There will be patrol officers outside of here for the day and into the night. This is when it gets very dangerous for you all. That includes you, Mrs. Eden." Will watched the elderly lady closely, seeing the understanding in her eyes. "We'll be back as soon as we can." Will ran from the house, heading for his car and then sped away.

Cavanagh leaned back on Cleary, feeling his chin resting on the top of her head. She felt the silence around her, silence that meant everyone was praying and that they would wait patiently or impatiently depending on the mood that was prevalent at the time.

Dagen searched the faces of those surrounding him. He nodded. This was it, he knew. He prayed for safety for the police officers and then for protection for his little group. He turned and walked away, a slump to his shoulders that Foley caught.

Foley reached for his daughter, holding on a little bit tighter and longer than he normally would. He walked away after his father, stopping for a moment beside Mrs. Eden. He nodded at her quiet comment before he turned to study his daughter. Foley could see that Cavanagh and Cleary were indeed a couple. He prayed that they survived the next few hours.

Cavanagh walked away from the entryway, heading for her office. Cleary walked beside her, reaching for her hand and then pulling her down onto the couch. His head bowed as he struggled with his emotions.

Will and James had split up, each taking charge of a group of officers. Will headed for the outskirts of town, past Mrs. Eden's house, as James headed for the downtown area. This was when it got dangerous for them. Yet they could sense the prayers that were being raised on their behalf.

The arrest and search warrants were served quickly and without difficulty. The arrogance of the leader had him thinking that no one would ever find him or arrest him. Edgar Eden refused to speak. He simply demanded his lawyer.

Will and James stood and watched the interrogation through the window. The men and women were talking, Will suspected in hopes of landing a plea deal. The list of offences against Eden continued to grow.

Will walked away at last, overwhelmed at the information that he had heard. Eden's son and grandson were involved far too deeply to get off with easy sentences. Eden had been in the construction business for many years. That meant a lot of work going back over everything. It would take weeks to delve into everything.

James came to find Will during the early evening. He dropped into a chair in front of Will's desk, his head dropping in fatigue.

"Did we get everyone?" Will wasn't sure if they had, the day had been that hectic.

"We did. It's over, Will. Thank God, it's over." James raised his head. "I didn't expect it to be Eden."

"Nor did I." Will looked down at the paperwork on his desk. "We need to find Cavanagh and Cleary."

"In the morning. We'll be here most of the night sorting all the paperwork out." James reached for some of the paperwork. "Where are you in filing this?"

"About halfway through, I think. There are a lot of people involved." Will stared down at the paper that he was holding. "I didn't think that we would arrest that many."

"I know. We arrested more than we planned but some of them would be released without charges. We just did a sweep of everyone that we found."

Early the next morning, Cavanagh stood on her front porch. The early morning sounds of late fall were just beginning. The sun had not yet begun its rising. She drew in a deep breath, sensing that their adventure was over. Cleary walked towards her, wrapping her into a hug and dropping a kiss on her cheek.

"Okay, sweetheart?" Cleary felt Cavanagh's nod against his chest. "We're done, I think with this. I got a message from Will. He and James are heading this way in about an hour or so."

"That's good. Dad and Grand are up. I think that I heard Mrs. Eden moving around. What are we to do for her? She helped us when she didn't have to."

"I know, sweetheart. We'll find something to do for her." Cleary turned Cavanagh back into the house, knowing that they would find the answers that they were praying for. "It's been a struggle to get to where we are. We have learned that God is with us at all times. He has led through this every step of the way. We don't like what we have had to face but we have never been alone. He has sheltered us and protected us. He has provided the keys to unlock the doors that we needed at the times when they were needed. I have learned to trust in a way that I never have before." He tilted his head to watch her. "And I found the lady who completes my heart. I love you, Cavanagh." Cleary bent to kiss her, finding her responding.

Will and James showed up a couple of hours later. They searched the faces of all the ones who had gathered in Cavanagh's living room and that group now included Jeff and his parents.

"What can we tell you?" Will drew in a deep breath. "We have them all, people. We have them all."

"Why?" Cavanagh's one question broke into the silence in the room.

"That we don't fully understand, Cavanagh. No one seems to know much other than they were given tasks to do under threat of assault or death. He blackmailed some of them to do his dirty work."

Mrs. Eden spoke up, the silence of the years broken at last.

"Eden is not a close relative of mine. I can tell you why. He was going broke and decided that he would use Cavanagh to break into homes and businesses for him. He is the one who led her to the Lockyer house. He then decided that he needed Cleary to do illegal surveys for him. Roger boasted about that after Cavanagh and Cleary were brought to my home. He didn't know that they were there. I was scare of him. I have seen over the years how he has gotten rid of people. Some of those suicides on the books are actually murders, I think. However his plans to use

Cavanagh and Cleary were to break into homes and rob them and then to lay claim to homes and businesses that he had illegal surveys for. These two people didn't cooperate. Roger claimed that the incident at the Lockyer house was an accident. I have my doubts about that."

Will and James were nodding. Mrs. Eden had filled in what they had not yet discovered. Eden was facing many years in prison. In fact, he would never be free the rest of his life. It would be up to the courts and crown attorneys to sort out all of the charges and who actually would be charged. Ivan Webster and Jane had been among those arrested. Even though it was still not totally clear as to who had been the abductors at different times or the whys it all, everyone was grateful that it was over.

Epilogue

Cleary was on a search eighteen months later. A year prior, he an Cavanagh had wed in a small ceremony at Mrs. Eden's home. They had decided that they loved one another and wanted to spend what time God gave them together. Foley and Dagen had been delighted with that.

Finding Cavanagh standing before the windows in a turret room, Cleary wrapped her into a hug and kissed her. Cavanagh leaned back against her groom, content to be held.

"Having a good day, sweetheart?" Cleary waited patiently for her to respond. She sometimes took her time to respond.

"I am, my love." Her face turned up to him. "You're done early today."

"I am. I have a big survey next but it will take more than the two hours I have left to work today. Jeff was not adverse to having some time off. He's working out so well."

"He is. He's a great kid. His parents are sweet." Cavanagh looked around the room that they had turned into an office. She had always loved Mrs. Eden's home. Mrs. Eden had suddenly decided just after the couple had married that she was ready to find an apartment and had simply signed the house over to Cavanagh and Cleary despite their protests. They had moved in not long after that but were still working to turn the house into their own.

“I spoke with Will today. He said that Eden finally pled guilty. We don’t have to face him in court.”

“That’s a relief. I was scared to do that.” Cavanagh hugged Cleary tighter. “God worked that out, didn’t He?”

“He did, sweetheart. It’s part of how He protects us.” Cleary was content to hold his bride. “We have so much to be thankful for.”

“We do. God has been with us every step of the way. It’s as you said. He had the keys to open the doors that we needed opened and to lock tight the ones that we didn’t need. That’s how He works.”

“It is. I just wish that we hadn’t had to go through what we did. But if we hadn’t, I wouldn’t be holding the love of my life.” Cleary kissed her again before he turned her to walk through the house. They had made it theirs and he was grateful for that. “Your dad and granddad are glad that none of us have to face Eden.”

“They would be. Dad asked if I still wanted to work.” Cavanagh had been slightly taken aback at his question. “I told him that I would. It’s not hard work.”

“No, it isn’t. It’s up to you. You are used to working. We can revisit it when we have a family.” He looked down as she blushed. He simply kissed her once more.

“We can do that.” Cavanagh moved restlessly for a moment. “I love you, Cleary. You are just who God had planned for me.”

"And I love you too. God has the keys to our lives. We just need to trust Him with them."

Dear Readers

Thank you for choosing to read *God's Keys*, the story of Cavanagh and her knight, Cleary. This story has been simmering for a while. But as always, the story was not what I had expected. The characters in the stories always go their own way. I, as the author, am only along for the ride.

Skeleton keys have always fascinated me. Growing up in an old farmhouse in the 1960s, we had doors that took skeleton keys. It was certainly a different time for locks on doors.

My father was a carpenter. At times, I would stand near him and watch him work. The old windows always had my interest. I would watch as he replaced the panes of glass, gladly kneading the package of putty that he used to seal the cracks around the edges of the glass.

That being said, what keys does God hold for us? We face closed and locked doors every day. Some of those He will open for us. Others He will not. That is where our faith comes in, to trust Him enough that He has our best in mind.

Emma Finlay showed up once more, albeit briefly. The story of Emma and Abe and his security team is found in the *His Guardian* series. They do like to show up in other stories. Blackie and Simon's stories are part of *Mistletoe Treasures*. Doug and Darcie's story is in *The Heart of a Lion*.

God bless each one of you as you walk your daily life. Trust God to know that He only wants the best for you. Let Him unlock the doors that He has planned for you.

Ronna

www.ingramcontent.com/pod-product-compliance
Lightning Source LLC
Chambersburg PA
CBHW070345200726
48294CB00003B/789

* 9 7 8 1 9 9 8 8 2 1 3 1 0 *